SPIKE

SPEED DATING WITH THE DENIZENS OF THE UNDERWORLD

BOOK THIRTY-ONE

ARIEL DAWN

NAUGHTY NIGHTS PRESS LLC• CANADA

SPIKE

Life was easier as a dog...

Cursed to be a Hellhound for all eternity, the last thing Spike expects is to shift back into a human on the steps of the DeLux Cafe in front of everyone, including his owner, Hecate.

Now he needs to learn what it is to be human in today's world, so he can pass for one himself and enjoy the offerings of humanity. Not to mention the fact he must find his mate before the next full moon or he will turn back into a Hellhound. After his life with overprotective godly guardians, going to college suddenly doesn't seem so terrifying.

SPIKE

When Spike discovers his mate on campus—a fiery vampire, no less—he finds himself in the middle of a hellish fairytale. The question is, will Isabelle be his happy ever after? Or will Spike's fate be sealed along with his human self for all eternity?

Spike is book thirty-one in the Speed Dating with the Denizens of the Underworld shared world, featuring a virginal hellhound turned human, a fiery vampire vixen, and more.

CHAPTER ONE

LIFE WAS EASIER as a dog.

Spike huffed heavy breaths, his shoulders tensed, his entire body flushed with heat as everyone stared. He hunched lower, trying to hide as he crouched—*naked*—on the steps to the lower level of the DeLux Cafe.

The voices that surrounded him belonged to those he'd come to know and care for deeply, those he considered practically family, though they hadn't the slightest clue he was a man cursed. A shifter trapped in the body of a hellhound.

"What the fuck..." Hecate's voice sounded above him, her grip on his leash tightening almost to the point of a choke.

Well, naked and on a leash is one way to make an appearance.

"Hades, did you—"

"No, I most certainly did not!" Hades's voice elevated, as Aphrodite and Eve clamored about what to do, because heaven forbid there were *patrons* just around the corner, and lord knows they didn't need the public—especially the mortals—to think they were some sort of sex club.

"Unhook him, Cate," Darcy's voice cut

in over the din as the cool air brushed over Spike's skin. It felt colder, seeing as he was now fully exposed and not covered with the comfortable sheen of fur he'd been used to for the last century.

Darcy knelt before Spike, her vibrant eyes catching his gaze as he tried to speak. But the words would not come.

Hecate knelt beside him, her fingernails scratching the edge of his neck as she unhooked his leash from his collar.

Spike's hand made its way up to his neck as he tugged on his collar for comfort, shaking his head back and forth, hoping she would understand, feeling the magical fabric expand for his much thicker neck. His wordless panic must have settled on her, as she pursed her lips, her spellbinding gaze softening as she pulled him closer, and he didn't fight turning his head into her chest, if only to shield himself from the heat of those questionable stares.

"Spike—" Her voice fell, laced with a thousand questions, a thousand things left unsaid, but it was the same voice he'd known for nearly a century. Her touch spoke volumes as she let her hand run along his back soothingly, warmly. Despite her outward appearance, and her natural venomous tongue, Hecate—or as she preferred to be called, Cate—was one of the kindest souls he'd ever met.

"Come on, let's get him somewhere more... private," Hades said, his voice taking on a much softer tone, but still commanding nonetheless. "We can use my office."

Hades grasped him under the arms and pulled Spike up. His legs trembled as the onslaught of everything crashed against him and he nearly stumbled in Hades's arms. Cate did not remove her grip from him either; instead, she ran her long fingernails along his skin in rhythmic fashion, much like she used to pet him when she was worried or concerned.

It felt more than strange to be stroked like this, not to mention to be upright on his legs, instead of bent over on all fours, and the light was blindingly bright to him with human retinas. The shift was unsettling.

Spike followed his caregivers, for his need to bow to their command was ingrained in him.

Hades had kept him for years, reaping souls, up until he'd been injured on a job, which was how he'd come to meet Cate. It was only supposed to be two weeks, but he soon found Cate to be a breath of fresh air, and was thrilled when she fell for the little dog and decided she had no intention of giving him back to his Master.

Spike shook the memories away. It was all quite disorienting as he fought to catch his breath. Only when the shutting of the door came, did he jump, recognizing his new reality as stern, warm hands helped him to sit in a soft chair.

Hades.

Cate ran her fingers through his long, disheveled hair with care, breaking the tangles that had formed, as he tried to still his rapid breathing.

The scent that he had caught on the edge of those stairs, sweet roses and lilies, that had thrown him into his unwelcomed shift was now gone, left out in the hallway of the DeLux's offices to dissipate into thin air along with the strawberry blonde who had caught his attention as she exited the cafe.

She was probably halfway across the city by now, and he didn't even know her name...

Mate.

The word reverberated in his brain. For it was the meaning of the word that spoke to him on such a deep level, called to the man within the monster and set him free.

"Go, grab him some clothes," Darcy spoke up, clearly the only voice of reason in the room amidst the awestruck Gods—well, technically there was only *one* God among them, since Hades had given up his godly powers—and Darcy seemed much better versed in dealing with crazy shit than the rest of them, being the only human to have both befriended a notoriously antisocial outcast, and to have bewitched the heart of one of the most powerful Gods of the underworld.

Darcy Little is a Goddess in her own human right.

"But—"

"No butts, H. He needs clothes, and probably a stiff drink—come to think of it, we could all probably use a stiff drink—and maybe some food, and maybe *then* we'll have a chance of getting to the bottom of... this," she said, her voice full of concern and command. "Whatever this... is."

Post-godly life had given Hades a new lease, and he found it quite difficult to "sit around all day" as he'd spouted to Cate during their last dinner visit. Spike had only visited his place of work once, when Cate and Darcy had decided to surprise the once immortal now man with a cake upon his new job.

It was still strange for Spike to see the normally flustered Darcy, so sure of herself nowadays, when she'd been the exact opposite up until...

Until she'd met her mate.

Spike turned his head away from Darcy and his former Master, in the direction of Cate, the woman who for the last century had acted as his Mistress. He stared up at her bright jewel-toned eyes with anxiety, the questions on the tip of his tongue as he tried to make sense of everything. She continued her soft strokes through his hair, her brows furrowing with as much emotion and question as he felt.

He'd tried so many times to tell her, for she was the Goddess of witchcraft, Keeper of the Wolves... surely she would have been able to discern or understand that he was cursed...

Cursed to remain beholden to an existence worse than an eternity in hell, to live as a hellhound, to hunt and reap the souls he'd vowed to protect when he was a young, cocky shifter soldier.

By a witch, no less.

"I'm so sorry Spike, I..." Cate's voice fell along with her eyes. "I didn't know I..."

"I know you didn't," he said, tasting words on his tongue, shocking them all.

Darcy and Hades turned to look with wide eyes. His voice was dry, cracked and deep. It sounded like the rumble of thunder in the distance of a desert.

Spike's tongue felt swollen, his throat dry as he curled himself into a ball in the lush, black velvet wingback chair in Hades's office, running his fingers over the spikes on his collar, the motion just as soothing to him as Cate's fingers in his hair.

"How could this have happened?" Hades said, running a hand over his face.

"Clothes, H!" Darcy bit, pulling the once-God out of his awe, and he did not think twice about moving.

"Clothes first, questions later! Spike

needs space to process everything..."

Spike turned to Darcy once more, his gaze catching hers.

"Darcy..." he said her name out loud, a whispered prayer.

Her eyes furrowed as she pursed her lips. "You're okay, Spike. I promise," she said softly.

The door shut and Spike felt like the world was spinning on its axis as a wave of nausea hit him.

"I—" Spike tried to form the words but they were difficult.

How could he accurately say what he longed to say, what he wished to say for so many years but could not?

How could he tell these women, both of them, what they meant to him, what their presence and their words meant to him now?

Exhaustion hit him as everything converged on him at once.

"I need..." he tried once more, but heat overcame him, as did exhaustion.

"Tell me what you need, Spike..." Darcy said as she knelt in front of him, settling her hand over top of his, pulling his attention to her.

"Yes," Cate commanded, her hands running up and down his clammy arm. "Start with what happened back there..."

Spike shook his head as he leaned into Cate's touch.

"Can't. Need..."

"What do you need?" Cate asked softly.

"Sleep..." Spike murmured as darkness fell, pulling him into the one place he had found solace as a cursed man.

SPIKE

His dreams.

CHAPTER TWO

ISABELLE STARED AT the sandwich board sign outside of the DeLux Cafe. The specials for the day were listed, and though most of them sounded appealing, she knew nothing would compare to what she truly hungered for—blood.

Though Eric and Nunez seem to swear by this place...

While most of her family were not so keen on blending in with the modern world, Isabelle Costanza was not about to let a little thing like blood stop her from experiencing the immortal life she'd been given to the fullest.

Starting with college, a job, and my own place far away from the estate.

She stared at the doors like they were made of holy water, when a woman with a rather large dog—a breed she'd definitely never seen before—waltzed past her in almost regal fashion.

She felt dizzy, almost rattled by the sheer proximity of the woman, as heat flushed her body, and her vision turned red...

The hunger for blood inside of her swelled, almost to a pitch in a way it hadn't since she'd first started the process of dieting. It had been nearly five years since she'd had a drop, and though she felt the occasional pang or craving for the sweet nectar, she'd never quite felt the *need* for it like she did at that moment.

The scent of fire and brimstone filled her airways, and it was thick and sweet, like honey, causing her heart to beat faster, and heat to blossom between her thighs. She was undoubtedly spelled by this sweet, intoxicating scent that she could not place, and so Isabelle pushed fear and caution from her mind as she chased after the raven-haired woman and her enormous black dog without a second thought, but they were nowhere to be found. It was as if they'd disappeared completely.

Her hunger ebbed, her mouth going dry, and Isabelle knew she needed to leave... for she'd chased the phantom woman and her dog into a pool of mortals. Mortals who did not smell nearly as delicious as the creatures who had passed her... the ghosts who left her standing. But that didn't mean they wouldn't cure her hunger. Mortal blood did not differ from person to person. It all tasted the same, and it never left her feeling whole or fulfilled, which was why she'd vowed to abstain from it. She did not like the monster she became when she chased the fiendish red nectar that would never be enough.

Just breathe. You can do this...

The scent of fire and brimstone hung in the air, luring her like a siren to jagged rocks. Or more accurately, to the stairs that descended into the lower level of the cafe, which her brother Eric had told her was where the supernaturals like herself were welcome. The thought of safety, of being far from the shark-infested waters of the mortal floor called to her, and she took one slow step forward. With every breath, she took one more step, following that scent until it disappeared at the top step. Disappointment filled her once more as she looked for the woman and her dog, nowhere to be found.

Her cell phone vibrated in her pocket, jarring her for a moment. She slid it out to see it was Lorelai, the only mortal on the planet who she did not wish to eat. The woman was as sweet and pure as they came, and had been a blessing as Isabelle stared at her map of the university on the first day of classes, offering assistance. The unease and discomfort she had felt as she openly stared at the new life she'd been so adamant about was almost immediately soothed by the woman, and though she knew it was improbable, Isabelle felt she could trust Lorelai. Trust had become respect, and respect had become friendship.

Isabelle decided at that moment that perhaps now was not the right time. Perhaps she was not ready to dive into the shadows of the DeLux Cafe, perhaps she was not ready to be thrown into any sort of romantic situations just yet. So she swallowed harshly, recirculating her brain to focus on the things she was certain of.

And as she tapped furiously at her cell phone, walking away at a brisk pace, she started to feel more like herself, as she walked back into the light of the outdoors, back into the safety of the world she knew.

***

The world was a haze of reds, ochres, and orange, and it smelled faintly of campfire. Like torched wood and smoke. There was a glow, a spark that caught her attention, dancing in front of her like a fiery pixie. The innate desire to follow the hellish wisp was overwhelming, and so Isabelle reached out to touch the magnificent spark. Only when her fingers came close to grasping it, it fell away.

She took a step closer, reaching out every time to get so close, but still she was so far away. Until she realized she was somewhere else. In a room full of plush booths and lined tables with numbers, a room for a party.

But where were all the people?

The room was empty, save for one table, far away. From a distance, she could tell the shadowy figure was tall, languid and domineering as he stood out against the red glow of the otherwise empty room.

Isabelle reached out to the spark, its outer tendrils tangling with her fingers at last. And then the world was blinding and bright as they collided like the sun, and there was nothing left but the feeling of pure bliss, sated hunger, and the scent of fire and brimstone.

"Wake up, sleepy head!" Lorelai shouted as she shoved Isabelle in the arm. The world around her was blurry and hazy, but much to her dismay, it was not bathed in red with shadowy, intriguing figures on the horizon. No, it was only filled by students tapping away on their laptops or snoozing in between classes like she had been.

"I'm up, I'm up!" Isabelle responded, rubbing her eyes. She could still feel the tingle in her fingertips as if the he spark had somehow left its mark.

"What is with you today?" Lorelai asked as she took a sip of her iced coffee.

"I don't know what you mean..." Isabelle said as she situated herself in her armchair, adjusting to the reality around her.

"I mean, you're always more awake than I am after Callahan's class."

"I'm just... feeling a little hungry, that's all," Isabelle lied. Lorelai, bless her mortal soul, did not even blink or think to press further. She was quite trusting for a mortal, a quality Isabelle felt was both endearing and far too dangerous. Which was why she'd taken it upon herself to protect the mortal at all costs. Someone needed to.

Like the best friend she was, Lorelai dug around in her backpack, producing a tart cherry yogurt-dipped protein bar.

Isabelle's lips tweaked up at the corner, the sweet gesture making her feeling a little better. She loved tart cherry, for it reminded her of the taste of blood.

"Thanks, Lora," she said quietly as she took the offering.

Lorelai smiled, the motion stretching her freckled cheeks and lighting up her bright eyes.

"I mean, what are friends for? That's the whole point, right? Having someone to take care of you and be there when you're hangry?" Lorelai said as she went back to her textbook.

Isabelle sank her teeth into the protein bar, relishing in the cherry bits on her tongue. The bite felt good, but it wasn't enough. It would never be enough. For Isabelle knew without the blood she craved, she would never be completely satisfied.

But she would have to keep living, anyway.

CHAPTER THREE

Three Weeks Later

"ARE YOU SURE about this?" Cate mused, her arm brushing against his. Gunner peered at him suspiciously from behind Cate, and Hades flanked him on the opposite side, Darcy curled around him like a second skin.

Spike stared up at the oversized clocktower of the University of Southern

California. He'd never been sure about much in his life, but the last few weeks since he'd awakened and shifted back into a human hadn't been the easiest. Though Cate and Hades had tried their best to help him adjust, neither of them understood truly what it meant to be human, not like Darcy or even Gunner did.

Cate had lived a reclusive life in the woods, running her animal rescue until she'd met Gunner—who Spike did not like in the least—but he wasn't entirely an animal either, being as he hadn't shifted until recently, something that made them closer in commonality than perhaps Spike would have liked.

Up until Hades met Darcy, he had been living a quiet immortal life, and had only recently given Darcy his soul. He was still getting used to mortality himself, and was not quite equipped in normal human behaviors like his whimsical mate was.

Which was why Spike relished having Darcy as a breath of fresh air. She was also closer to his age than either of his guardians.

He'd been poked and prodded by the Goddess and former-God, and even the pain in the ass shifter and the Fates as to his hex, his curse. It seemed the witch who had cursed him had frozen him in the hellhound state, which meant his physical body had not aged since he'd been cursed at the tender age of twenty-one. At least, that was the words from the Fates when Hades and Cate had taken him to be seen.

The spell that had been cast on him

was an old one; the only way to be cured completely was to be kissed by his mate who had awakened him, and bite them. A kiss and a bite of death—now that he had shifted. And as if that wasn't difficult enough, the reversal would have to be performed by the red moon, which by Cate's calculations was only a month away.

"I'm absolutely sure," he said as he swallowed his nerves.

The decision to attend The University of Southern California had been entirely on a whim.

In the past few weeks, Spike had taken to helping out his owners—

Except they are not my owners. Not anymore...

It seemed the change in Spike was just as monumental for Hades and Cate as it was for him.

Though Gunner doesn't seem to have an opinion unless it's Cate talking.

He'd been helping Cate and Darcy at the shelter, where he'd seen the commercial on the television for the university. The commercial wasn't anything spectacular, but it was the woman in the far right corner toward the end, who sat with her red-headed friend on the bench that drew his attention.

He knew it didn't make a lick of sense, it wasn't like he could see her face, just her long, strawberry-blonde hair that covered her, hid her from the cameraman.

But the sight caused his blood to heat, his cock to twitch, and his heart to race.

Perhaps it would be easier to just... go

back to the cafe, he mused as he stared up at the clock tower. The campus was crawling with people—most of them young in appearance, like himself—though Spike couldn't help but feel a sense of panic and anxiety as he looked at them all. Talking, chatting, laughing.

The world had changed so much since the last time he'd been upright on two legs.

No, Spike knew regardless of the fact his mate was out there, that he needed more.

He needed to learn the ways of modern humanity, and the best way to do so was to observe those who were closer to his frozen age.

To pass as a normal twenty-one-year-old man, he would have to learn how to be one. And perhaps in that search of knowledge, he would find *her*.

The one who awakened me...

"What're you waiting for? Christmas?" Gunner chirped, drawing Spike from his wandering thoughts. He pursed his lips, shooting the lumbering shifter a scathing look.

"I'm sorry, Gunner, did you forget your nap today?" he nipped.

Darcy giggled as Hades sighed, and Cate shot her mate a look that would have terrified an army.

But only Gunner was stupid enough to roll his eyes.

I'm sure he'll pay for that later.

"Last I checked, big boys don't need their hand held to go to fucking college." Gunner snarked.

Cate's eyes glowed as Gunner stood his ground.

"What? He's a grown man, he doesn't need us—"

"He's literally been a person for like three weeks, asshole. Cut the kid some slack," Darcy nipped.

"Whatever. You all want to play Modern Family, that's fine, but I think I saw a keg over there..." Gunner said as he pushed away from the wall of solidarity, heading off into the distance.

Good riddance, asshole.

"I have no fucking idea what you see in that brute," Hades said with a whistle.

Darcy poked him in the ribs, and suddenly the tension in the air melted.

Cate pulled Spike closer, wrapping her arm around his waist. The touch was comforting, and Spike couldn't help burrowing into her hold. He'd always found his mistress attractive, but he'd never felt an attraction to her.

In all the years she'd fed him, walked him, cuddled him, not once had he wished it was more. He'd only wished she could understand him, that perhaps she could break his curse so he could be with the living again as he truly was. He'd only wished to experience life the way he was meant to, not as a soul-reaping animal whose archnemesis was an annoying black cat.

"His bark is worse than his bite, truly," Cate said with a smile. "The important thing is we're *all* here for you, Spike. Should you need us." The implication in her words, combined with the almost watery gaze, softened his heart as he recalled many a time Cate curled around him for comfort.

Like the night Gunner showed up and

she'd shut him out.

The memory pushed forth of his mistress who sat against the door in tears, grasping at his neck. His gaze held hers for a long moment, her jewel-toned eyes looking almost as if she was about to cry.

Spike felt Hades squeeze his side, the motion instantly putting him at ease.

Hades cleared his throat. "We're only a phone call away."

"Thank you," he said calmly as he picked up his duffel bag once more.

"Do you want us to come with you?" Darcy asked, her voice lilting in excitement.

Spike turned to look at her bright eyes, her lips curved in a smile that made her look almost childish.

It would have been very easy for him

to say 'yes,' because like Cate and Hades, Spike trusted Darcy, felt better with her around, but he knew he could not bring her with him, and if he was to make a good impression on entering his dorm room, he knew it would be best to leave his parental figures on the lawn.

Not to mention there's no way I can explain what or who they are... No, it's better to leave me on this side of things, so as not to complicate matters further.

I need to do this alone.

"No, I think I got it from here," he said, as he took a step forward.

"You have our numbers," Darcy said, her voice wavering with sadness.

"If you're having second thoughts—" Cate said, her solid tone full of despair.

"If I need you, I know where to find you."

Hades pulled Darcy back, and Spike pressed forth, one step at a time, refusing to look back. Instead, he looked all around him, watching everything he could. The cheerleaders practicing, the young adults smoking and browsing their phones, the...

Immediately, Spike's ears twitched, his sense of smell picking up the faintest scent of roses and lilies on the wind. The scent made his blood boil, his skin flush with heat. His cock twitched as his mouth watered, and his heart raced, feeling like an animal who'd just caught whiff of their prey.

And perhaps, that was all the more this *mate* was to him. Prey to hunt, a soul to reap. After all, you couldn't teach a dog new tricks.

You're not getting away from me this

time...

A deep growl escaped his throat as he slung his duffel over his shoulder and embarked on the hunt.

CHAPTER FOUR

ISABELLE HUFFED IN annoyance as Eric chortled in her ear.

"Patience is a virtue, Iz," he said in that matter-of-fact tone of his, as he watched a young teal-haired collegian skitter past them with interest. Izzy ground her teeth.

This was a bad idea.

While most of her family didn't seem to care for her rebellious nature and would have rather drank holy water than acknowledge her choices in life, Isabelle's brother was in fact the closest friend she'd had growing up in the Constanza's regal coven.

Well him, and Nunez of course. That guy is like attached at Eric's hip.

Though like most of her kind, Isabelle, Eric, and Nunez were not *actually* related. They only shared the name of their coven, but for all intents and purposes when her coven had resettled in the Los Angeles area, they'd kept the illusion of a wealthy family. Ricardo and Camilla Constanza were truly the head of their coven, but to the mortals, they were parents to Eric, Isabelle, Thalia, and Jose. Though their rumored to be haunted Los Angeles mansion was home to many more vampires than just the six of them; after all, those who lived in the hills among them frequently had staff coming and going—which was why the Constanza Coven had chosen the real estate to begin with.

All the better for snacking, and no one will bat an eye.

"I told you, the mortals are off limits here," Isabelle griped as she hit her brother in the arm.

"Oh, but they look so tasty, Iz. I don't know how you resist..." he said as he licked his lips, his fangs protruding. "Come on, just a little fuck and a bite?" he groaned as another woman walked by, catching sight of his gaze. The blush that crept across her face made Isabelle roll her eyes.

"You promised, Eric," she whined like

a petulant child.

Eric sighed as they both stepped forward to order their coffees.

"What'll it be?" the bored, amber-eyed student droned, her eyes glazed beneath the shade of the ballcap she wore that read, *Wake The Dead Coffee*. Isabelle had been appalled by the name at first, mostly because of the coffin and coffee logo—many things shocked and awed her during her first semester—but she'd had a year to become acquainted with the happenings of university life, and thus, not much surprised her anymore.

So why do I come back?

"I'll have a large Edward, please," Isabelle said, her brother looking at her with a raised eyebrow.

"Didn't peg you for a Twilight fan, Iz," he guffawed. "College life must be rotting your brain."

Isabelle flashed him a glare.

"I'm not. But it's white chocolate raspberry with whip cream and cherries, and you know I'm a sucker for cherries."

Eric grinned, the motion of his lips curling back to expose his fangs, a sight that would have been attractive to her if not for the fact she knew Eric preferred his bloodbags with a dick.

Something they had in common.

"And for you, tough guy?" the student drawled sarcastically, her eyes just as dead as the tone of her voice.

Perhaps she needs to drink some coffee herself.

"Large Vlad for me, please. No sugar, no cream."

Isabelle wrinkled her nose. "You are disgusting. It's basically sludge at that point.”

“Some things in life don’t need to be dressed up, you know. Some things, *good things*, are perfect in their own right,” Eric said as the cashier rung them up, and they moved down to the counter.

And then a familiar high-pitched squeal caused Isabelle’s blood to chill, and her entire body froze.

“Hey Izzy!” Lorelai said with excitement. Eric’s gaze caught hers, and he smiled wickedly.

“And who is this beautiful specimen, hmmm?” Eric said as he sauntered toward Lorelai. Isabelle threw her arm out, stopping him in his tracks. Just a slight nod of her head and the barest exposure of her fang was enough to tell her brother this one was off limits.

"Oh, I... uh... didn't realize you were with someone," Lorelai said with a blush, her gaze flitting back and forth between the two of them.

"Oh, this asshole? No, we're not... um, he's my... brother." She wasn't sure why lying to Lorelai felt so awful, she only knew that she hated to feel as if there were any secrets between her and the mortal.

Eric raised an eyebrow at her, his smile peaking at the corner of his lips. He reached his hand out across the bar of Izzy's arm, extending his hand to Lorelai in a polite gesture.

"Eric Costanza, at your service, mon cheri," he said as he took Lorelai's hand and placing a swift, chaste kiss on the back of it.

And then it hit her... Amidst the

wafting scent of decadent grounds, was something else. Something much darker, earthier.

Isabelle's entire body reacted to the scent of fire and brimstone like a lightning rod. She turned her head, looking every which way she could, but it was no use. The crowd in the cafe outside of the university library was far too crowded. It was, after all, the start of the new semester.

The familiar scent made her stomach twist, her mouth water, and her fangs *ache*. The overwhelming desire to find the owner of the scent was far too difficult to fight, and Isabelle did not think.

She only acted on impulse.

"Izzy, you okay?" Lorelai asked, her voice etched in concern.

"I—"

"Iz…" Eric's voice also carried an air of worry, though Isabelle couldn't fathom *why* her friends were acting so strange…

"Grab my coffee, I'll, uh… I just—"

The intoxicating scent was stronger now, and it was too hard to resist.

Isabelle's legs carried her quickly toward the library, her entire being driven by one thing only.

Hunger.

No iced coffee or protein bar would do, either. No, this hunger was for something so much more.

She was aware of Eric and Lorelai behind her, following her. She knew she would have to fabricate some sort of lie for her mortal friend, and perhaps one for her coven mate as well.

For how could she explain to either of

them that she smelled a scent so strong that it enticed her appetite in more ways than one.

For heaven's sake, when she'd escaped it the last time, she'd been so hungry, so aroused...

Yeah, definitely not telling Eric that. I'll take that to my coffin.

And so, Isabelle followed the blood song, the hellish scent of burning embers down through the stacks, her vision red with hunger and lust.

If I don't find them soon, I think I may be forced to—

As her mind wandered and her vision blurred, the scent practically infiltrated her lungs. Her body had gotten warmer, almost as if it were on fire, and—

Smack!

It seemed Isabelle had become

distracted.

So distracted, she'd walked right into a solid, lean mass of limbs wearing black ripped jeans and a white shirt.

"I'm so sorry, I—" His voice disappeared in the wind as she looked up at him. Dark hair fell in his glittering gold eyes, and it was like the world around her had fallen to pieces.

The scent of fire and brimstone wrapped around her like ribbons, heating her from the inside out, this man—

No, this is not a man, this... this is something else.

A supernatural.

Like me.

The man from my dreams...

Though Isabelle was certain she did not know many supernaturals outside of the vampires in her coven, except for demons and the occasional angel. But this man did not exude a demonic or angelic air, nor did he *smell* like a demon or angel.

Isabelle blinked, looking around him for the woman she'd seen at the DeLux, but she was nowhere to be found.

But the scent—that mouthwatering, intoxicating scent was still there. It did not dissipate.

Perhaps...

"No, my apologies, I uh... wasn't watching where I was going..." Isabelle spoke, her voice shaky, as if she hadn't been spoken in years.

The man looked down at her, his pink tongue darting out to lick his lips, and she could have sworn she saw a flicker of red in his fiery gaze. She blinked, but it was not so. There was only the deep, amber glow that reminded her of burning embers.

"Are you lost?" he asked, his voice deep and full of darkness, his hand settling on her hip to provide support. The touch was gentle, almost cautious, but Isabelle couldn't deny the warmth she felt where he touched her, as if he himself were fire incarnate.

Isabelle felt the weight of his question like a steel beam. His words were simple, but somehow they evoked a response within her she could not deny.

For his words were predatory, taunting in the way a hunter would coax his prey into the sunlight to be slaughtered.

And something about that both terrified Isabelle, and intrigued her all the same.

"Not all who wander are lost," she murmured, biting her lip. Her fangs ached, and her entire body felt flush with heat.

What the fuck is wrong with me?

"And you are..." Eric's voice cut through the fog that had befallen around them, and Isabelle shook her head. The man dropped his hand from her waist, taking a step back, and the golden haze in his eyes disappeared.

Perhaps I am losing my mind.

Perhaps this is what happens when one goes too long without blood consumption.

"I, uh..." the man spoke, his voice much gentler and youthful than only moments ago.

It was like he was someone else.

"My name's Lorelai, and this here is Isabelle... I mean *Izzy*, and—I'm sorry, I didn't catch your name—" Lorelai said as she flashed her dimples at Eric.

"It's Eric, darling."

"Isabelle..." the man said, his gaze falling back to her where she stood. The way he was looking at her made her feel quite on the spot, and she carefully pulled her hair to cover up the blush in her cheeks. For the way he said her name was like a wish, an unanswered prayer.

Like she herself were some sort of Goddess or powerful witch.

It was then she noticed the man in front of her was wearing a collar. A dog collar to be exact, with silver spikes, and his long, lithe fingers seemed to be stroking the metal in a fashion Isabelle recognized too well.

Fidgeting.

The man was nervous.

Probably a freshman.

"This is the part where you say 'hey, my name is—'"

"Um... people call me Spike."

"Of course they do," Eric drawled, a light chuckle escaping his throat. Lorelai handed Isabelle her coffee.

The coffee she'd forgotten about when—

"Are you staying on campus?" Lorelai asked, steamrolling through the awkward tension like the force she was.

"I am, actually. My dorm is right over there," Spike pointed out the window on the right side of the room.

"You all checked in?" Isabelle asked, remembering how to speak, finally.

Spike nodded. "I... didn't have much to move in, and I figured I should get acquainted with my new surroundings."

"They never do," Lorelai hummed.The way Spike spoke... wasn't quite right. His tone was off.

Isabelle could feel Eric's gaze at her back, and she knew she'd likely hear about this for at least a month.

"Do you have plans?" Isabelle said, blinking furiously.

"Who, me?" Spike asked, looking around, almost as if he expected her to be talking to someone else. But there was only the four of them in the corner of this aisle, right outside of Dr. Leehan, the history professor's office.

CHAPTER FIVE

SPIKE'S HEART RACED in his chest as reality set in.

He'd followed the scent of roses and lilies like a bee to honey, narrowing his tracking abilities he hadn't called upon in years.

Instinct took over, guiding him like a beacon as he made his way through the crowds across the university lawn, down and around the sidewalk, the scent getting stronger with every stride until…

Until he'd blinked, finding himself in the university library of all places, face to face with *her*.

At the DeLux Cafe, he hadn't been able to get a good look at her; what with his entire world view being lower to the ground than his current form, not to mention the fact he'd barely had a moment to contend with what was happening, as shortly after he'd gotten a whiff of his *mate*, his entire world shifted. Literally.

Everything had happened so quickly, he could barely process it, and in many ways he still couldn't process that this—standing on two legs, sleeping in a bed, going to college—was now his life when he'd spent so many years as a soul chaser. A retired soul chaser, to be exact.

When he'd caught the tiniest glimpse of her strawberry blonde hair in the cafe, and then again in the commercial... he knew he needed to find her. If only because her scent drove his animal wild in the same way it coaxed his true beast out of its hellhound prison in a way he'd never imagined. He'd felt quite literally, torn in half.

But none of those glimpses were anything compared to the woman who stood before him. She was of average height, with fair skin that reminded him of the peach tones of the inside of a seashell.

Her hair cascaded around her shoulders in soft, strawberry blonde waves, framing her face like a golden halo. Her lips, perfectly pink and open just the slightest, the sight of the tiniest sliver of fang coaxed his inner animal to the surface as thoughts raced through his brain about just what they'd taste like against his own, what it would feel like to run his tongue along the sharp, pointed edges when her fangs were fully out to play...

Vampire.

His mind settled on the word, even though he hadn't seen a vampire in near a century, since before the evil witch had cursed him.

At that time, vampires were dark, ravenous creatures who wreaked havoc wherever they wanted, with no allegiance or no loyalty to anyone, or anything other than the blood they chased.

And Spike, in his effervescent youth as a soldier of the Great Athena's army, had hunted more than his fair share of monsters. Including vampires.

Though he knew such a thing should have horrified him, he found it hard to think of anything else except the vixen in front of him. His insides rippled with anticipation.

Perhaps this mate will be able to set me free, to break my curse...

His cock stiffened in his jeans at the thought, weeping along with his soul to covet the beautiful creature him, and finally be *free..*

The word was more than clear, the reality tangible at last.

So why could he not move?

After all, was this—was she—not the very reason he insisted on attending the university?

The glimmer of hope that he would

find her, that she would truly break his spell... it was all happening as he wanted, so why did he feel so frozen, so... afraid?

All at once, as the man behind her spoke, Spike remembered where he was, and that despite the tunnel vision this vampire procured within him, they were not alone. There were civilians, many of them. And he did not know this woman, this vampire, beyond her scent, or the truth of the bond he could feel tugging beneath his chest.

Isabelle.

Her name is Isabelle.

Spike blinked, realizing Isabelle was waiting for his response, as he looked around the room, settling his gaze back on her..

"Me?" he asked, feeling as if his brain

and his body were warring with one another. His animal longed to shift, to sink its fangs in the perfect expanse of *Isabelle*'s neck and reap her in an entirely new way.

His animal wanted her *soul*. He wanted to feast on her like a damn buffet.

A bite of death.

The fates had been clear that the only way to break his curse was with a kiss and a bite of death. But he needed to be smart. He could not go about biting the woman in the light of day in front of such a crowd.

Not to mention, he had other wants and desires that did *not* revolve around the prospect of his... mate.

He did desire education. To learn what it was to be human in today's world, so that he could well pass for one himself, and enjoy the offerings of humanity.

His life in Athena's army had not been the easiest, and education was not as abundant for those like him, at the time. His options were limited, since he was untethered, and untrained. While shifters were not uncommon, there hadn't been any record of a shifter like him.

Most of the men in Athena's army could shift into wolves, or large cats, and even Athena herself could shift into an owl.

But no man had ever shifted into a creature of hell, and that was the reason Spike walked alone. *Demons have no place here,* his mother exclaimed as she had shut the door in his face. He was not, by definition a *demon*, though he understood how one could make that assumption. There was nowhere for a penniless, broken, lonely hellhound shifter to go except the Goddesses's supernatural army.

His wants, desires, everything paled in comparison to feeding the animal who drove him.

The very animal that drove him to the den of the witch in the first place, seeking retribution from his inner beast.

I had been too trusting then, and I will be damned if I make the same mistake twice...

"I uh... no, not really. I'm kind of new... here... so..."

"You should come with us to the kickoff party," Isabelle—no, *Izzy*—as the redhead, Lorelaid had introduced her as—said.

"A party?" he asked, blinking away the confusion.

A party would be large, would it not?

Perhaps it was not safe, nor a good idea to put himself in the mix with his mate and so many others.

Not when he knew he wanted *less* people. The need to get this sinfully dangerous creature alone nagged at him, and he fought to ignore it.

I need to build her trust first. She may be a vampire, but I doubt she'd be open to letting a man she just met bite her.

Then again, a party would be a wonderful place to observe the student body. I could learn much from this...

"Yeah, you know, alcohol, loud music, stupid Greek shit."

Spike tilted his head in curiosity.

Did this vampire just insult his home?

"I will have you know that Grecian intelligence is far superior to—"

"The Alpha Pi Beta assholes have no intelligence. All their brain cells were traded for muscles," Izzy said as she brushed her hair over her shoulder, her voice full of sarcasm and disdain.

How dare she!

"Perhaps I can join as well?" Eric asked, his voice edged in curiosity. Spike noticed how this man's tone made his *mate*'s entire body tense. Instinctively, he tensed as well, taking an involuntary step forward. The need to defend, to protect within him stirred like a hurricane.

But such a reaction was crazy, wasn't it?

After all, he didn't know this *Eric,* didn't know who he was to Isabelle.

Was he her lover?

The thought caused an immense pang of jealousy to ebb within him.

Perhaps, this will not be as simple as I thought...

"Oh, I mean... I don't think it's really your kind of thing..." Isabelle said as she turned her gaze away from Spike for the moment. Eric grinned wickedly.

"I'll bring Nunez. He loves parties," the man taunted her, his bright eyes sparkling with mischief.

Not to be outdone or forgotten, Spike spoke with haste.

"This is fun, for you?" he asked.

Izzy cocked her head to the side. "It beats sitting alone in my dorm like a loser," she said, puffing her chest and her words out like some peacock. Spike did not miss the glimmer in her eyes, or the way she licked her lips.

"I like to be where the action is," she said darkly.

"Then I will be there," he said matter of factly.

Isabelle pulled out her phone, her gaze barely breaking his as she tapped away before handing him the device. Spike looked at it in question.

"I'm sorry what... are you doing?" he asked.

"Put your number in, I'll text you," she said, her tone only a little judgmental.

Spike bit his lip as he slowly reached out for her phone. Darcy had insisted on getting him one almost immediately after they'd discussed where he was going to reside for the time being.

After much deliberation, Hades relented to accept Cate's offer to let him continue to live in her cabin on the edge of society. It was after all, the place he'd been living—albeit as a rescued, cursed hound—for a century. Not long after the visit to the Fates, Darcy and his keepers had taken him on a sort of shopping spree. There was nothing out of their reach—money was truly no object for Hades or Cate, despite their appearances and the way they lived. He'd gone home with more clothes than he was certain he'd ever wear, as well as modern day technology Darcy insisted 'everyone had', including a cellular phone and a computer, a laptop as she called it.

But Spike had not taken to the technological advances of society quite as easily as Darcy would have hoped.

Spike stared at the screen for a moment, noticing that it was already cued up in contacts, the cursor blinking in the sliver of white space where one would type a number.

You can do this. You can type numbers, for heaven's sake.

He took the phone gingerly from her hand, his fingertips brushing against the edges of her sharp nails. The touch alone caused heat to race through his body, and he could feel his knot starting to swell. He knew he needed to get out of the library, and find...

Find somewhere to take care of this problem... but where can I go?

He sucked in a breath, as he held her phone in his hand, trying to remain in control of the situation, focusing on tapping out those tiny numbers he'd been drilled into remembering.

Only when he completed the task did he let out a breath as he handed the phone back to Isabelle.

"Sweet, I'll catch you later, Spike," she said with a grin as she turned around, following her friends out of the library, leaving Spike hard, alone, and wondering what the hell he'd just gotten himself into.

***

Spike blew out a breath of relief when he found his humble abode empty.

It seemed as if perhaps, for once, the Gods were on his side.

Though he wasn't certain when his roommate would be back, he couldn't focus on worrying about such things at the moment, not when his knot was driving all his attention, and his inner beast was raging for release.

He'd been so close...

Since his initial transition into human flesh once more, he'd more than reacquainted himself with his cock and his desires, but even in those few, lonely moments he hadn't felt quite this desperate, this full.

He'd barely made it out of his pants before locking the door to his side of the suite, if only out of self preservation.

The last thing he needed was a human to walk in on him and his very un-human cock, with a full, swollen knot, which was starting to feel rather uncomfortable.

Even among the soldiers of his youth, he knew he was an anomaly. None of the other shifters in Athena's army boasted equipment similar to his own. It was only after he'd been to a party—thrown by the domina he was tasked with protecting alongside a few other select soldiers—where the demons fucked their hostess in a voyeuristic display had he discovered there were indeed *other* creatures with his... enhancements.

And those creatures, were creatures of hell. Demons.

Spike laid back on his rickety bed, slamming his back against the wall as he wrestled to free his cock from the constraining *briefs* he'd taken to wearing beneath his new clothes.

The cool air kissed his sensitive skin as his heavy cock bobbed free, a fresh bead of precum at his tip gleaming in the light. His cock throbbed, hard like solid marble, aching for warmth, for release. For his *mate,* who was not there..

But such a thing was crazy wasn't it?

To be so worked up over a woman he'd literally only just met?

Spike swallowed in defeat. It was no use combatting logic when all his faculties were being pulled along with the blood in his body to the insurmountable desire culminating in his knot.

His eyelashes fluttered lazily as he took in the sight of his purple, swollen knot, his mouth going dry as he wrapped his hand around the base, letting his thumb gently brush over the bulbous swell that hat gotten big enough he could barely wrap his fingers around it.

The tingle in his knot from the touch was somehow both relieving but also not enough.

If I get this worked up from just grazing her, how the hell am I going to get close enough to bite her?

Just the moment of letting his thoughts wander was enough. Enough to remember the sparkle of her eyes, that perfect shade of blue-green that reminded him of ancient petinas on elaborate statues.

The memory of her perfect, pink lips, parted just enough to see the edge of her fangs stirred his beast's hunger.

He longed to bite those plump lips, to feel the plush skin between his teeth, to taste her blood.

The momentary thought of her blood in his mouth caused his cock to spurt a fresh stream of wetness, which only made him ache more. He groaned in desperation, squeezing his cock tightly as his fingers rubbed the leaking liquid along his engorged shaft and knot. His desperate thrusts made the mattress squeak, the rickety wooden frame groaning in response as his movements came in harder, faster.

Images filled his brain of sweet, tender flesh, the scent of lilies and roses filling his airways as his fantasy took hold, and he imagined Isabelle beneath him like prey as he feasted on her flesh in more ways than one, the thought making his entire body heat like *hellfire.*

The bed creaked as his knot burst, a deep growl escaping his throat. Warm, sticky spend shot forth like a geyser, coating his abdomen, his thighs, his trembling hand, the force a barrage of relief. The world around him fell away like a landfall as he plummeted from the mountain of pleasure, back down to the confines of the small isolated dorm room where his body shuddered from the intensity of his orgasm, the warmth of his blood and release giving way to the chill, stale air of his bedroom once more, dissipating like snowflakes the moment they hit a solid surface.

Immediately, he felt the onslaught of guilt, of embarrassment and worry.

He could hear the sound of doors opening and closing, and he knew his moment of solitude was over.

And sooner or later he would have to contend with the woman his entire being longed for, the woman who could finally break his curse.

If only he could keep himself together long enough to do so.

CHAPTER SIX

YOU ARE OUT of your fucking mind, Iz.

Izzy nervously sucked at the remains of whip cream and cherry sauce through her straw, if only to calm her frayed thoughts.

Being a vampire, by its very definition meant that she exuded an air of lust. It wasn't as if she had never garnered the attention of an attractive man before. In fact, she had become rather bored with the attention she usually received. It was commonplace, a part of immortality.

All the better to lure the mortals in so I may feed...

But there was something different in the way *Spike* looked at her. His fiery gaze, the flecks of gold glittered with hunger that called to a part of her she hadn't known existed until she stood in front of him.

For in Spike's gaze, Isabelle felt the unimaginable.

She felt like prey.

Every part of her predatory nature rattled against her human cage, her blood rushing like a tidal wave and awakening a desire deep within her, not to just feed, but to *bite*. To mark this man, this creature of unknown origin as *hers*.

Which was ludicrous, considering she barely knew the man.

Logically, Isabelle knew she should steer clear of such a creature. For if Spike was able to cause such a reaction so quickly, so vehemently, it was probably best she keep her distance.

Trust no one, Isabelle, Camilla had told her, all those years ago when she'd been a scared, newborn darling brought into the Constanza's home. Ricardo had been the one to find her, dying of blood loss in an alley behind the tailor's shop in Spain. He'd sealed her wounds with his venom, trapping her in immortality in the process, but Isabelle was remiss to fight him as he feasted on the mess her attacker had made.

At the time he'd found her, she had only been the second to be be sired by

Ricardo, a notion his *mate* Camilla did not favor.

Though despite her icy beginnings in the coven, Ricardo had never treated her as anything other than an equal. He'd never tried to seduce her, nor had he tried to persuade her in any way shape or form. He'd told her she could stay or she could have gone, the choice was hers.

But why would she want to leave the trappings of the coven when it was all she'd desired?

A warm bed, a closet full of finely tailored clothing, and every luxury she could ever want was at her disposal, if she would only pay the price.

And that price was blood.

It was a quiet life of blood and lust, one that left little room for desire of anything else.

But blood, like any other currency, could be corrupted.

And Isabelle had found herself too trusting in her youth—a feat which had brought her to that alley where she lay dying in the first place.

Camilla had taught her to trust her instincts, and those instincts hadn't steered her wrong over the centuries...

But was it trust or lust she felt for the mysterious supernatural who made her blood rush and her entire being flourish with heat?

He was certainly attractive, but there was something else, something she couldn't quite place...

All she'd known at that moment was eventually the moment would cease, and he would disappear, and that she could not bear.

So she did the only thing she could think of, and invited him to the kick off party—which would not have been such a bad idea had it not been for the fact that Isabelle herself had never been to the Alpha Pi Beta house or any of their parties.

It wasn't like she'd never thought about attending the parties on campus, but she'd always wondered if she'd be able to truly resist feeding on mortals in a setting such as a party. With copious amounts of liquor and throngs of sexual encounters, Isabelle wondered if she'd be strong enough to resist those pulls.

Guess we'll find out tonight, won't we?

Isabelle drained the last of her drink as she waltzed in her shared dormitory, alone.

ARIEL DAWN

It was Lorelai's night to work at the Leehan Gallery, though she did not anticipate much of a rush to the dusty old gallery, especially with the place closed for setting up their next exhibit, some mythological thing.

She hadn't been paying attention when Lorelai or their manager slash adjunct faculty friend, Calli, had briefed them on it.

Isabelle did not take her work-study job quite as seriously as her friend did. After all, she'd lived through too much of history to subject herself to the mistruths and gilded lies the history books peddled.

She was much more a woman of science, than art—which was why she'd chosen to study Molecular and Computational Biology instead of

Painting like Lorelai.

Though her job working at the Leehan Gallery would look lovely on a resume if she decided to pursue an actual career at some point in her immortal life.

Despite the fact he was nowhere near her, Isabelle could not shake the heat. It was almost as if her insides were like a volcano, hot, molten lava culminating just below the surface.

No sooner had she thrown away the plastic cup, was she disrobing, seeking the welcome chill of the air. Slick sweat had started to form underneath her breasts, behind her knees;, not to mention the warmth spreading between her legs. A creature of blood, Isabelle was not so used to being *hot.* Her natural temperature ran cold, even in the warm LA sun, on account of the vampire venom in her blood.

Which was why the heat was as frightening as it was delightful.

Nothing, and no one had ever made her feel like *this*.

She turned the shower handle on as cold as it would go, wasting no time as she jumped into the small space. The spray of the chilly water kissed her skin, and she could actually hear a sizzle as it hit her skin.

But it wasn't enough. The water could not cut through the heat that blossomed in her core, that emptiness that echoed to be filled.

Isabelle leaned against the cold tile wall, the instant temperature shift against her back a welcome sensation as she slid her hand down her abdomen, her fingers trailing warmth across the sensitive flesh of her swollen clit.

The touch was minimal, but it sent a shockwave through her core. Instinctively, she whimpered, desperation clouding her vision and judgment. She needed more. Truth be told, she needed her blue and purple dildo that was inconspiciously hidden in a JoyBox under her bed, but she was afraid if she left the confines of her icy cold shower, she would surely burst into flames.

No, it seemed there was only one way out of this fire, and that was through.

So instead, she imagined Spike and his fiery eyes above her, holding her in place, and she imagined him filling her as her favorite toy usually did. She imagined as she slid two fingers into her warmth, the stretch she'd become accustomed to; the thick, marbled silicone knot that accentuated the base of her custom sex toy was the perfect height and weight to grind her clit against.

Though Isabelle had been with mortal men over the years, she'd never found the experience particularly memorable. It was usually over rather quickly, and until she'd invested in the KnottyDX5, she hadn't truly experienced the bliss of a fulfilling, toe-curling, earth-shattering orgasm.

"Those monster romance books are going to rot your brain," Lorelai had told her far too many times, but Isabelle could not get enough of such things. For the truth was far worse than fiction.

Even lustful creatures like herself, as

beautiful as they were, were still at the crux of it all, monsters.

Killers.

Spike certainly looked dangerous, but she felt in her bones he was the farthest thing from dangerous. The fire in her body spread as she became far more lubricated, just from the thought of Spike like one of her fictional boyfriends.

All hard muscles, thick cocks, and knots full of...

Isabelle let out a relentless groan as the fire in her grew, her fantasy taking flight. She imagined her wet, slippery fingers grasping onto the metal spikes of his collar as he took her, filled her until that delicious, fictional knot burst.

She knew it was insane to fantasize about a man she'd only just met, especially in the way she was, but something about that only aroused her more. It wasn't like he possessed the necessary equipment anyway. No man or creature that she knew of possessed such things. That was the fun of fiction.

But despite the fact she knew it could not be, she let herself imagine the possibility. And when she finally reached the peak, when she'd fully imagined Spike burning her with his gaze while he speared her, filling her to the brim with her darkest desires and dreams, only then did Isabelle feel eternally free.

CHAPTER SEVEN

SPIKE PACED BACK and forth in front of the library. At this time of the night, the place was closed, but it was one of the only places on campus he seemed to be able to find without a map.

Because it was only a five minute walk from his dormitory.

He had no clue what one wore to a *Greek* party, which he had learned in the several hours since meeting Izzy, was not actually a party held by Grecians themselves as he thought.

No, it would seem the Greeks in question were actually referring to college students who pledged their names to organizations of brotherhood or sisterhood that were lumped together into sororities and fraternities that took on names inspired by the Greek alphabet.

Which still did not tell him what sort of attire was appropriate, but Spike digressed.

His expensive black jeans with the holes in them and his form fitting black v-neck shirt and black Converse, Cate bought him, would have to do. As he waited, he absentmindedly stroked the metal of his spikes on his collar, wondering if perhaps the fair vampire of his desires had decided against this intrepid youthful right of passage.

But just as he considered turning back around and heading back to his dorm, he caught her intoxicating scent on the wind like the bloodhound he truly was. His heart beat a little quicker, his cock stirring with interest as he focused on Isabelle walking across the courtyard. Thanks to his shifting capabilities, his sight was much better than the average human or even the average shifter.

Isabelle emerged from the darkness that had fallen across the campus, dressed in a red velvet dress with black lace accents. It was a short dress, coming to just above her knees, and the neckline was adorned in black lace, though the dress itself looked poorly cut. For starters, her breasts were barely supported, bouncing heavily as she strode toward him. Her long hair had been swept up into a high ponytail that cascaded down her fair back, her patina-colored eyes rimmed in black, making them stand out all the more. His cock twitched as his gaze settled on her ruby red, glossy lips.

The sight reminded him of blood, making him all too aware of the blood rushing to one particular spot of his body...

"Wow," he murmured, completely taken aback by the beauty of such a divine creature. Beneath the moonlight, she looked every bit an otherworldly being.

"You look amazing," he said, trying to recover.

"Thanks, I guess," she said

swallowing harshly.

"Where are your... friends?" he asked, his heart racing as he realized she was alone.

Not that he wanted anyone else, except her, but the reality made his anxiety swell.

"Lora had to work over at the gallery. Calli, our boss, is off on a tangent about the upcoming exhibit. Eric is... otherwise occupied."

Spike noticed the way Isabelle flinched as she mentioned her male friend. Protectiveness swelled within him.

Had Eric hurt her somehow?

"So it's just us," he said warily.

Isabelle shrugged. "Unless you got better plans, Spike, looks like that's the case."

"I've never been to a party before," he admitted as he sunk his hands in his pockets. Izzy strolled past him, leading him along a path he was not certain would not lead to death itself.

But a part of him felt death by a creature as beautiful as this one would not have been a terrible way to go.

But would the curse let him?

If he did not get the kiss or bite of death, what then?

Would he be damned to be a hellhound for the rest of his life?

Without thinking, he caught up to Izzy's pace rather quickly. Her wild rose and lily scent wrapped around him, luring him once more.

"There isn't much to it, I'm afraid. Shitty music, even shittier alcohol," she said sardonically.

"You... are of age, right?" she asked as she stopped for a moment, her gaze roving over his form. Her jeweled eyes glittered against her pale skin, making her look almost ethereal.

"Of age to..."

"Drink? I mean, just so I know if I should run away from your fine ass when the cops show up."

Spike couldn't help the smirk that curved at the corner of his lips. The bite in her tone wasn't menacing or degrading. It was playful. Flirtatious even, and that gave Spike a boost of confidence. His anxiety dissipated a fraction.

"I am twenty-one, if you must know. This is the legal age of alcohol consumption, yes?"

Izzy looked at him as if he'd grown

two heads.

"What is with you? You sound like a person, but your linguistics are... off."

Spike's smirk soon disintegrated into a frown from the realization that perhaps he'd said something wrong.

But last he checked, twenty-one was the legal age to drink, and technically it wasn't a lie. He was still twenty-one... in his human form.

He'd been sealed into his dogged form on his twenty-first birthday.

"I don't know what you mean," he said as she rolled her eyes, taking off for a darkened corridor between two buildings he didn't quite recognize yet.

Though as he followed Izzy down the alley, his animal instinct flared.

He moved faster, reaching out for her hand. She startled as he took it, nearly jumping off the ground.

"What the fuck—"

"I'm sorry, I just..."

Izzy pulled her hand away, her gaze fixing him to where he stood.

"What's the matter? You afraid of the dark?" she teased, but he could see the shimmer of glowing aqua in her eyes, the heaving of her chest as she tried to cover up her reaction.

And he could certainly feel the heat from where her palm had touched the back of his hand, his skin still flushed from her touch as if she were made of pure fire.

Spike regarded her with a cautious look.

"Perhaps I should lead," he said.

Isabelle crossed her arms, the motion drawing attention to her ample cleavage.

Spike felt his inner animal lunge forth, his proverbial hellhound tongue practically hanging out of his mouth as he noticed the stiff peaks through her velveteen dress.

Which told him she wasn't wearing a bra or any sort of support beneath the soft, pillowy fabric.

His cock twitched as images filled his brain, of sliding those black straps over her shoulders, of letting her breasts free. Of the goosebumps that would certainly form over her skin, the chill taste of her cold skin in his mouth as he warmed said stiff peaks with his tongue...

He shifted his stance, trying to push away the thoughts. His cock protested, his knot already starting to swell from the thought alone.

Now is not the time!

"Perhaps you should not," she said sternly as she turned, continuing on her way, and he followed her without question.

***

"This is—" Spike said as he stared at the large house with ornately designed columns, reminiscent of the homes he'd seen as a shifter soldier. Despite his rank and his talents, Spike hadn't been at the top of his regimen. He'd been on the lower run, doing mostly security work for those who sought assistance and protection from Athena. While the Goddess herself was quite the soldier, she had a bit of a soft spot for those who needed protection. A true heroine, she was.

Spike found himself wondering as he

looked at the front lawn of Alpha Pi Beta if the Goddess was still around, and if she would be the same warrior he once knew.

Or perhaps time had changed her as well.

"Yup, this is it," she said as she stopped beside him, just as another student whizzed past them, stumbling and sloshing their drink all over Isabelle.

Spike caught her as she stumbled on her heels from the motion.

The moment his fingertips brushed against her arm, he felt a jolt of electricity.

The world around him fell away as images accosted his mind of things that didn't make a lick of sense. Of Isabelle, wrapped in glowing blue tendrils, on the other side of a large, spacious room.

The tendrils of magic flowed around her like ribbons, as one word echoed in his subconscious.

Mine.

His entire body felt like the earth moved beneath his feet as he held her, helping her to stand upright. Her big, blue-green eyes called to him and his inner beast.

He licked his lips and his own fangs attempted to push through his gums, which pulled him from the reality of the situation.

Regrettably he pulled away as Isabelle stood on her own.

"Fucking assholes," she mused as she nodded toward the front porch.

"Well, come on, then, let's go make some bad decisions," she said with a grin as she headed for the door.

"Of course," he mumbled as he followed her into the unknown.

***

Spike drank down the remainder of the liquid the modern youth tried to pass off as beer.

I've had beer, and this soapy water is not it.

Though he couldn't deny that it was doing *something*. He felt more relaxed, more at ease for the moment as he sat on the stone pavement next to Izzy.

Isabelle swung her bare feet in the shallow water of the pool, clutching her red cup. She'd been staring at it for near an hour, but she hadn't made much of a dent.

"Are you okay?" he asked, a little too loud. One of the *Greek* sisters looked at him with disdain as if he'd interrupted some dire situation.

Though from the cackles and the other sound effects coming from the woman's group of friends, he rationed she would have given anyone the stink eye, had they done the same.

"I thought... I thought it would be worse than this..." she murmured absentmindedly.

"Ouch, way to make a guy feel good, Izzy."

By the Gods, did I just say that out loud?

She turned her head to face him, the motion causing her long strawberry blonde ponytail to fall over her shoulder, over her round breasts.

The water reflected on her from below, making her look positively angelic.

"It's not you, it's just... I avoided these things for a long time," she said quietly.

"What's a long time?" he asked curiously. "Are you graduating or something?"

Izzy looked thoughtful as she considered his words.

"Or something," she said as she stood, Spike following her motion.

That was when the DJ finally came back from wherever the hell he'd gone, queuing up another song Spike didn't know.

He hadn't gotten a handle yet on all the music, as there seemed to be quite an abundance of it.

Darcy had given him a list of bands to listen to, but he'd barely made a dent in it.

The song had good rhythm, and he was feeling much more comfortable from the several cans of beer he'd consumed. He shifted his hips back and forth as he built his own rhythm, swaying back and forth in repeated motion as he closed his eyes, letting the music move him.

Even with his eyes closed, he could feel the vampire's steady gaze, like a target.

And perhaps in a way, that was what they were to one another. Moving targets.

Though Isabelle hadn't given him any indication she wished to strike, but he knew he had to be careful. Vampires were generally very skilled hunters, but nothing beat the hunting skill of a hellhound.

Vampires themselves could track blood, but did not hold life in the palm of their hand. As a hellhound, a creature of hellfire itself, Spike was gifted with the skill of reaping. Though in Hades care, he'd reaped plenty of souls, it never felt much like a hunt. Not when there wasn't much of a fight in reaping what rightfully belonged to the Underworld, to Hades.

When he opened his eyes, he saw bright, vibrant oceans staring back at him.

Isabelle placed her hand on his hip softly, tugging him toward her.

"You are a terrible dancer," she said with a smirk.

"We need to work on your bedside manner, Izzzy," he said darkly, his voice much too husky even for his own liking as he rolled his z's endlessly.

"Maybe you just need a good teacher," she purred in response as she gently tugged once more, urging him to follow.

Spike set his hand on her hip, relishing in the feel of the velvet between his fingertips.

"Perhaps, I do," he said as he pulled her closer.

Isabelle rocked her hips, swaying back and forth as she pulled him with her, and he met her rhythm. Slow, steady, and sensual, they moved together like lock and key. Isabelle ran her hands up his sides, his shirt catching in her grasp as she tugged at the fabric.

Spike slid his hand back in a moment of bravery from his liquid courage, resting his palm above the small of her back as he pulled her against him. The touch sent sparks through his entire system, his hound rising to the surface, just below his skin.

He was so very hungry, and Izzy looked like warm cherry pie on a golden platter.

The sight of her beneath the moonlight, in his arms on the edge of the pool was like a dream brought to life, and the way she was looking up at him was too difficult to ignore.

His cock twitched, eliciting a sliver of a cross between a whisper and a moan from Isabelle's ruby lips, her fair cheeks pinking with a blush that made his heart race.

A part of him wanted to be embarrassed at his sudden erection, but all thoughts of embarrassment faded into the air as Izzy drew her lips to his ear, the heat from the friction of her velvet dress against his tight, jean-clad arousal like a drug all its own.

"Careful, Spike," she warned, her breath on his skin warm and enticing. Her hands slid up his sides, over his chest, and up his neck, fingertips toying with the edges of his dark hair, and Spike knew he was surely doomed.

Because despite her warning, despite knowing that everything about this situation and the woman in his arms was dangerous, he knew the undisputable truth.

Isabelle would be the death of him, one way or another.

And perhaps a kiss from death was exactly what he needed, and so Spike did not waste another breath, as he found his courage, and dove off the cliff into Isabelle's dark waves.

He only prayed he would come out alive.

CHAPTER EIGHT

ISABELLE HAD NEVER felt so helpless in all her life. The magnetism that surrounded the mysterious Spike—whose last name she didn't even know—was irrefutable. He possessed an otherworldly air, and the way he spoke was reminiscent of another time, but the tone of his voice, the clothes he wore, and even the light in his eyes, were unequivocally youthful.

It was almost as if he was a dashing man of another time, trapped in the body of an attractive twenty-one year old.

Who couldn't dance to save his life.

Spike tightened his hold on her, his palm settling at the small of her back as he gazed down at her with deep, golden eyes that reminded her of the setting sun. His gaze stirred an innate desire in her to fall and let the heat he brought upon her consume them both.

What the hell is happening to me?

I'm not usually like this...

Spike's body moved slowly as he followed her rhythm. The amber light from the string lights above them cast an incandescent glow on him, making his skin look almost as golden as the glow in his eyes.

Isabelle's mouth went dry and she clutched his arms tightly, if only to ground herself to the present reality that Spike, was indeed a dangerous creature.

And she needed to be careful or she would end up ruined.

Her fingernails dug into his skin, right over his skull and flames tattoo, something she hadn't noticed before.

He gently tugged her closer, until their bodies were pressed together like dried flowers between the pages of an old, forgotten book.

Isabelle could not fight the blush that formed on her face as she felt the repercussions of their proximity against her, nor could she fight the heat that had started to spread once more between her thighs.

It took all of her concentration *not* to

whimper in defeat, to not grind herself against Spike's rather sizeable erection twitching against her.

To not sink her fangs into this dangerously delicious creature and devour him on the stone pavement in front of the entire campus.

"Careful, Spike," she warned, though she was not sure if such a warning was meant for him as much as it was meant for herself.

Because in the presence of tall, dark, and collared, she felt like an animal in heat.

Spike stroked her sides warmly, his touch separated by the hot, red fabric a maddening sort of torture.

Isabelle removed her hands from where they clutched his arms, traipsing her fingertips up his soft, white shirt, relishing in the smooth texture of solid muscle there as well. The desire to touch him everywhere, to mark the landscape of his skin with her bite was damn near overpowering.

Sweat had started to form once again beneath her breasts, and the heat in her core was like a volcano, the apex of her thighs already moist from desire.

I need to get the fuck out of here before I do something...

Just as her breath hitched, her heart raced, Spike did the unthinkable.

He leaned in closer to her, his lips only inches away from her trembling ones.

Isabelle wanted nothing more than to be captured by his lips, to fall into the dark, unexplored waters that would surely drown her if she was not careful.

But she could not bring herself to submit to a man she barely knew, a man who held such power over her.

"I think I need some air," she breathed, her voice full of lust and desperation. She pushed herself away from Spike and his intoxicating fire and brimstone scent, not even bothering to pick up her shoes.

"Izzy—" Spike called her name, and she hated how *sweet* it sounded on his tongue. Her bare feet slapped against the stone pavement as she ran off, through the backyard toward the main drag of Greek Row.

When she finally found the pathway, she followed it, Spike's footsteps behind her catching up quickly.

"Just don't," she said, hating how her voice cracked as she refused to look at him.

If she didn't keep moving, she'd never escape his gravitational pull. She would be consumed.

"I'm sorry, I didn't mean—"

Isabelle stopped, the sounds of Greek life but a whisper as she realized they'd run clear off the beaten path and were now alone, in the dark in front of the clock tower.

The night was still around them, the faint hum of Alpha Pi Beta like elevator music.

"I said don't!" she bit as she turned around, taking in the sight of Spike once more. His dark hair hung in his golden eyes, and he had the audacity to look *hurt*.

How dare he make me out to be the bad guy!

"You can't just show up out of nowhere and... and... ugh!" She could not for the life of her, find the right words to explain the confusion, the attraction, or the frightening heat ransacking her every time she got close to the mysterious man.

"You can't just show up here and sweep me off my feet like some fucking fairytale. That's not how this works," she hissed, her fangs on full display.

Most sane men would run at the sight of the unnaturally pointy pearly whites, lest they were already lured and dead in the water.

But Spike's eyes only *glowed* with ferocity and golden light as he exclaimed, "Me? My life was a lot easier before I met you, Izzy, I can assure you. You can't just fall into my life like a shooting star, make me shift and—aaaagh!"

Isabelle watched in horror as Spike's entire body *rattled*, as if something was trying to force its way out from beneath his skin. His eyes glowed as he clutched his chest, his fingertips shaking as claws formed at the edges. He hissed at her, exposing long, bright fangs.

Shifter.

Spike is a shifter...

The sight alone, mixed with his heady fire and brimstone scent terrified her. Because she knew as the sweat soaked her dress, as the harsh reality presented itself, that she was right. Spike *was* dangerous.

Because he wasn't just a shifter, he was a shifter bred from hellfire itself. He was a hellhound shifter, and there was only one thing those demonic creatures wanted.

Souls.

Isabelle's eyes furrowed as she hissed back, several years of stocked vampiric rage rising to the surface.

Spike fought with himself, a deep roar escaping him as he turned away from her, and Izzy did not waste the chance. She used his distraction to fade into the darkness, and escape once more.

CHAPTER NINE

WHEN SHE'D FINALLY made it back to her dorm, she was running on adrenaline. Though it seemed despite the late hour, she was in fact alone.

That's strange, usually Lorelai is home by now.

Almost as if the woman was psychic, her phone pinged with a fresh text.

Staying over at Calli's tonight. Fill you in in the morning on the way to Painting.

Isabelle tossed her phone on the desk, running her hands through her soaked hair. She was still a hot, sweaty mess, and her mind was racing with all that had happened.

The memory of Spike's lips inches from her own, of his sizeable cock grinding against her, of his maddening touch, separated by the fabric of her dress.

She couldn't deny she hadn't been aroused by all of it, and even now in the privacy of her room she couldn't deny the effect it had on her just to *think* about it.

About him.

She'd wanted to kiss him.

She'd wanted to *make him hers.*

But he was a shifter, and not just any type of shifter. One who could destroy her immortal soul.

Hellhounds reaped souls for the Underworld, a task that truly was the mark of death, even for someone like her.

Even monsters had souls, despite what the books and movies said.

The memory of his *fangs*, that ferocious growl...

Not to mention how he'd fought with himself...

Isabelle couldn't help but think perhaps there was more to the situation.

Regardless of what had happened, Spike hadn't *hurt* her.

"No, don't even go down that route, Iz," she said with heavy breath as she removed her dress. The cool air was welcome against her sweat-slicked skin, and she slid her panties off, noting they were *drenched.*

"Oh for fuck's sake," she groaned. Her legs were slick with arousal, and she whimpered in defeat.

What sane creature gets turned on by another monster?

And one that could kill me nonetheless?

The thought alone caused a fresh wave of desire to tear through her.

I am so fucked up.

Her gaze caught the edge of her JoyBox, stuffed behind the drape of her black comforter on the ground in front of her bed.

Her pussy throbbed with need, knowing there was only one way to combat the heat Spike brought out in her.

Just get off and get him out of your

head.

Isabelle did not think twice as she reached for the only thing that would dull the ache, the pain and quiet the thirst that had formed in the back of her throat.

Within mere seconds, she had positioned herself just so, sinking down easily on the long, thick length in one swift motion. Her insides throbbed as she hit the base, the thick, bulbous knot that sent a shiver through her as it brushed against her swollen, wet clit.

Isabelle rocked her hips against the stand-in, trying to focus on anything but Spike.

But nothing, not even the thought of her fictional men would do. Her release was so close, yet so far, and she whined in defeat as she chased her elusive orgasm.

Yet when the memory of his fiery gaze forced its way in alongside his cock twitching, his sweet scent and his pouty lips, Isabelle could not fight it, or the blinding bliss it brought. She closed her eyes tightly as her walls closed in on the KnottyDX5 and its thickness, knot and all.

The stretch as her insides quivered was too much. Never in all the time she'd used the device, had she been able to take *all* of it. And she'd been content with that, relishing in the sensations it had brought her without coveting its entirety.

Isabelle buried her head into her pillow as she bore down on the toy, her muffled screams of frustration and ecstasy like a macabre waltz.

When her breathing finally returned to normal, Izzy dismounted, feeling guiltier than she'd ever had before. She only hoped that when she showered, she could wash away more than just sweat.

***

The light poured in through the window, directly on Isabelle. She groaned in response. It wasn't that she burned in the sunlight—such a thing was made up by Hollywood to make her kind seem easily defeated—rather, she despised the light when she felt ill, as she had this morning.

All night she tossed and turned as thoughts of Spike and their disaster of a night tumbled through her brain. From his touch to his near-shift, to her blinding orgasm.

She was certain of two things—the first was that there was something clearly wrong with her. Never in her immortality had she felt so strongly about anyone, the way she felt about Spike. Especially when she was in his presence.

The second was that she needed to be practical, logical. Staying away from the sexy shifter who made her entire body heat from his touch alone, was probably a good idea.

It should be easy, right?

This place is huge, what are the chances I'll run into him?

CHAPTER TEN

"WHAT DO YOU mean you almost shifted?" Cate asked, panic in her voice evident.

Spike ran his hands over his face. He could feel the judgment rippling off Gunner, who loomed grumpily in the corner of Hades's office.

"I don't know what happened. One minute we were dancing, and the next—"

"We?" Hades asked, his deep voice

cutting through the chaos of Cate's panic.

Spike let out a breath before speaking.

Better to just get it all out and in the open...

"Her name is Izzy..." he said quietly.

"Oh for fuck's sake," Cate bit, Gunner's laugh slicing through the tension in the room like butter.

"Oh man, you've been a college student for what like a day? And already you're getting laid?" His whistle angered Spike.

"It's not like that!" he said, feeling the rush of anger igniting his inner hound. He rose from the chair he'd been sitting in, his hound's spirit *rippling* beneath his skin in the same way it had when Isabelle... hissed at him.

When she showed him her deadly fangs.

Cate took a step back, her eyes fixed on him, as Darcy called out, "Don't listen to him, Spike."

"Shut the hell up, Gunner," Hades nipped, his tone full of command and authority. Gunner only had the audacity to roll his eyes, as if he was not afraid that there were at least two people in the room who could flatten him like a pancake if they wanted to, and one of them was newly mortal.

"It's a compliment, *H,*" Gunner bit back. "Lighten up."

Spike's shoulders relaxed as his hound settled a fraction, leaving his heart still racing from the burst of shifting energy.

"Besides, it's a normal reaction. It's

the mate instinct taking over," Gunner said with a shrug.

"But you never shifted," Darcy pointed out. "So how do you know?"

"Not until I found my mate," Gunner said more seriously, his dark eyes falling on the raven-haired Goddess in front of him.

"But believe me when I tell you, my animal was *begging* to be set free when I was in her presence," he said, the tone of his voice tinged with a gravely dark edge.

The responses of 'gross' and 'oh my Gods,' echoing from Hades and Darcy would have been more comical to Spike given any other situation.

While he didn't care for Cate's *mate*, he knew there was no denying their actual bond. The one the diviner had unearthed, the one that had pushed

Cate over the edge and broke through her guarded walls.

And the way Cate looked at the pain in the ass shifter across the room, stirred a longing in Spike's own soul.

It reminded him of the way Isabelle looked at *him.* Before she ran into the night, before they'd argued and shown their true colors.

Mine.

Mate.

The words didn't matter as much as the intrinsic, deep seeded understanding hit Spike like a cannonball. Perhaps his hound knew what he did not wish to acknowledge to his pseudo-guardians.

"She ran off. And when she left, I—"

"Came back down to earth?" Gunner asked, raising an eyebrow.

"Something like that," Spike

admitted.

"This woman, this Izzy..." Hades started as he slowly paced the room.

"You think she is your... mate?" Hades said the word plainly as if it did not hold the magic every one of them in the room knew it did.

"I... don't know," Spike responded, unsure of what to say. While he knew in his heart the answer was yes, he also knew that unless he obtained her kiss and bit her, his days were numbered, a feat none of his present company could comprehend. Their mate bonds were founded without curses or expiration dates.

Why is this so damn complicated?

Gunner grunted in the corner, and Cate cast him a vicious glare.

"What? I didn't say anything," he bit.

"Perhaps you should stay away from this Izzy, until you know more," Hades said calmly.

"Until we *all* know more," Cate said definitively.

"Of course," Spike said reluctantly. Just the thought of not seeing Isabelle, of not touching her, or being wrapped up in her sweet floral scent made his hound anxious.

And so Spike nodded in agreement as Hades opened the door, ushering out Darcy and the Goddess first. Gunner sauntered slowly after his mate, flashing his gaze at Spike for a moment before he exited. Hades held his hand up to stop Spike from his leave.

"What time are your classes done tomorrow?" he asked solidly.

Spike sighed, blowing some strands

of dark hair out of his face. "I think my last class is done around one," he answered.

"I would like you to come by my office tomorrow after your last class," he said.

"Why?" Spike said, feeling a sudden surge of anxiety.

Had he done something wrong?

It wasn't as if he could *control* what had happened... or if it would happen again.

"Gunner may understand the instinct to shift, but you are a rare breed, Spike. You are not just a run of the mill shifter, you are a creature of hellfire. And I know more about hellfire bonds than anyone else," he said as he nodded in the direction of the empty hallway.

The implication was not lost on Spike. After all, he'd spent many years under Hades's Mastery, therefore he'd seen firsthand the bond the former God of the Underworld had formed with Persephone.

He'd also watched the pain of that bond ignite and consume Hades until he was nothing more than a charred heart.

Until he'd found Darcy, that is.

Spike nodded in understanding as he walked through the door.

The DeLux Cafe was empty at this time of the night, or was it morning?

Spike was not entirely sure, and that was when exhaustion hit him.

"Now, get some rest. You have a long day ahead of you," Hades said as he closed the door behind them.

***

When Darcy had helped him pick his

classes, he hadn't quite the idea what it was he wished to study. His only desire to attend the university stemmed from his need to find his mate—the one who had been responsible for engaging his shift—Isabelle.

Which was why he hadn't thought twice when Darcy had placed him in Painting 101. Though he had to admit, as a young man in Athena's army, he'd seen his fair share of art. The Romans were rather fond of it, after all.

But aside from eraseable doodles in the dirt, Spike had no inclination or natural affinity for art. However, that did not mean he could not learn from the Masters who would be teaching his class.

He'd just settled into his seat when the scent of lilies and roses hit him.

Immediately, his cock twitched, his heartbeat quickened, and his hound awakened as he turned around so fast he thought he'd get whiplash.

Isabelle's deep ocean eyes stared back at him in shock as her redheaded friend, Lorelai, tugged her arm to follow her.

What were the odds they'd be attending the same class together?

He watched, frozen in his place, as Izzy followed her friend to the other side of the room. While their drawing desks were scattered about the room in an arch, the cavernous studio felt rather intimate.

A pedestal draped with fabrics in the center of the room boasted many items of varying decor. Antique tea cups and saucers, vases, and strangely shaped glass sculptures caught the sunlight filtering through the windows, causing tiny prisms to dance across the room like pixies.

His gaze followed Izzy and her mesmerizing, lithe body as she glided across the poured concrete floor like an angel on clouds, her dark wash jeans hugging the sinful curve of her backside, making Spike's inner hound salivate.

And then she turned away from him, breaking the spell she had on him.

Finally, the professor arrived. While the syllabus papers cited her as Calliope David, she insisted on being called 'Calli', which Spike felt was rather informal given the woman's obvious title of professor.

Though as *Calli* droned on about the history of painting and its mark on the world, Spike could barely concentrate.

Or more accurately, he could not concentrate on anything except the work of art who refused to look at him.

Memories of their prior evening replayed in his mind like a movie. Her fingernails digging into the fabric of his shirt, the way she ground herself against his hardness, the heat of her breath on his skin.

The way she called his hound to the surface, the way that one word repeated over and over in his mind.

Mine.

Spike's mouth went dry and he licked his lips.

Could he stay away?

Could he resist the woman who held the cure to his curse?

The desire to possess and bite her

was prevalent, now just at it had been the prior night.

For a moment, he'd thought he had her. That as he leaned in to take her lips among his own, she'd leaned in too.

It would have been so easy. His lips crashing against hers, tongue tasting her with a newness that could never be repeated.

And when she leaned in, he'd let his lips wander away from her delicious mouth, to tender flesh.

It would be quick, and painless.

Just a pinch.

A kiss, and a bite of death, and then he would be free.

But just the sight, the thought of Isabelle, caused his hound grave unrest, and despite the fact she was across the room, looking at anything but him, his entire body longed to be near her, to touch her. To hold onto her and never let go.

"All right, that's it for today. I'll see you tomorrow, and we will begin our first project," Calli said excitedly, some of her dark hair falling out of her messy professor bun as she clasped her fingers together. The sea of students filtered out of the studio, and Spike did not think.

He only acted on impulse as he rose, making his way through the crowd like a salmon swimming upstream, but he did not have to go far. For it seemed that Isabelle was just as fired up as he was.

"I'll catch you later at the Gallery," Lorelai said, casting her friend a knowing glance.

I wonder what that's about.

When the redhead had disappeared,

and the rest of the room had dispersed, Spike realized they were indeed, alone.

While his hound and his cock most certainly had ideas of their own of what to do with the vampire in his clutches, a deeper notion propelled him as her intoxicating scent filled his airways.

While he wanted nothing more than to taste her kiss, her blood, he also longed to please her. Quite simply, he wanted her to *like* him, and he had not done the best job so far.

"Hey," he said nervously as she stopped in front of him, her arms crossed tightly. The motion drew his immediate attention to her breasts as the position smashed them together.

"Hey," she said, twisting her lips.

"I, um... listen, Izzy... I—" he stammered as he ran a hand through his dark hair.

Why were the words so difficult to say?

Something shifted in Izzy and her stance, in her demeanor that moment. It was as if whatever walls she had constructed, flickered, and her gaze of annoyance turned softer. Sweeter.

"Spike, listen—"

"I didn't mean to... scare you. I didn't mean to make you uncomfortable, in any way if I did, I just—"

"What makes you think I was uncomfortable?" she asked with a raised eyebrow. Spike looked back and forth curiously.

"Um, you ran away from me when I—" His voice caught in his throat.

Isabelle smiled wickedly and the sight caused his cock to awaken once more.

You are not helping matters!

"I thought maybe you... liked me... and what we were doing."

Isabelle must have picked up on his discomfort, and like the vicious vampire she was, dug her fangs in deep. She did not relent.

"And what do you think we were doing, Spike?" she asked, her tongue clicking on the k in his chosen name like a time clock.

She was playing with him. Flirting with him.

He shook his head, all too enticed to follow her down the road again, but he needed to be honest with her. Her mood swings, her push me, pull me attitude was giving him whiplash.

"I don't understand you," he whispered, his hound chomping at the bit to close the space between them, to run his hands along her sinful frame and—

"You don't understand me?" she said as she cocked her head to the side.

"What's there not to understand? I'm a vampire, you are a demon, and—"

"I am *not* a demon," he said adamantly.

"You are a creature of hellfire, are you not? Is that not demonic by definition?"

Spike shook his head. "Do not change the subject. Since I have met you, I have not been able to get you out of my head, and just when I think maybe you feel this—-whatever this—" He pointed between them furiously. "—is, you get cold feet and you shut me out."

Isabelle's eyes softened.

"I am not shutting you out, I just..."

She clicked her tongue, running it along the edge of one of her fangs. The sight caused his cock to throb, and heat to flourish beneath his skin.

"I don't even know your last name," she whispered, even though there was no one in the studio to hide their words from.

Spike looked at her with sadness. For the life of him, he could not remember his first name, let alone his last.

So he gave her the only name he'd known since he'd forgotten his own.

"Moon," he said Cate's moniker easily, smoothly as if it had always been his too.

"Spike Moon," she repeated the name softly, tasting it on her tongue.

"Sounds like a rockstar or something," she tutted as her shoulders relaxed.

"Last night, when I—" He swallowed nervously. "I think, somehow we got off on the wrong foot, Izzy," he breathed her name like a prayer.

And perhaps in a way, it was. For he certainly wished he could start over, avoid his mistakes.

Isabelle twisted her lips, her jeweled gaze roving over him.

"It's not you, Spike," she said with a deep breath. "It's me."

The way in which she could not look at him as she said the words struck a chord deep within him. The need to soothe her worry, to make her feel better was as potent as the tingle in his knot that had started to form.

"I've never seen... or been close to another supernatural creature other than my own kind before. Not since I was—"

"Bitten," he said, understanding just how deep her fear went.

Of course, how could he have been so blind, so uncaring toward something so obvious.

Isabelle may have been a vampire, but she hadn't been one all her life. At some point she was *bitten*.

And what did he wish to do?

His eyebrows furrowed and he bit his lip as the words out of his mouth poured out of their own volition.

"If it makes you feel any better, I've never been this close to a vampire before—"

His voice trailed off as he realized the words he was about to say would likely be an axe to whatever shred of hope there was that Isabelle would let him in, that she would save him. So he swallowed the words down quickly and changed direction.

"Like this, I mean," he whispered as he moved an inch closer.

Isabelle's body relaxed, but she pretended not to notice.

How do I earn your trust, Izzy?

"What do you mean?" she asked, her own voice a trembling whisper as she moved in closer, close enough he could feel her warm breath on his skin. And just like the prior night, the magnetic draw he felt in her presence—the way her scent surrounded him, the way his heart raced and his blood rushed, the way his animal *begged* to be free as Gunner had suggested—was a powerful, heady cocktail.

Isabelle's breaths shook as she stared up at him with glassy eyes, her fingertips teasing the edge of his shirtsleeve as if she too wanted to give in, but could not find the courage to do so.

Spike reached his hand out to push back some of her golden hair that had come loose from her ponytail, behind her ear. The tiniest touch of his fingertips along the sensitive skin made his entire body heat like a burning fire.

"Tell me you do not feel this— energy—between us. Tell me... tell me I am wrong and I will leave you be for the rest of eternity."

Izzy licked her perfectly pink lips, her eyelashes fluttering as she let out a deep breath.

"It's not that simple, Spike," she said as she closed her eyes, turning her head away.

"But for the record, I wish it was," she said as she moved away. Her voice carried the hint of sadness, and Spike felt it in his bones.

"I have to go, or I'm going to be late for my lab, I'm sorry," she said as she left him standing alone with the undeniable truth.

That without her heart, he was a goner.

CHAPTER ELEVEN

SPIKE WALKED DOWN the shadowed corridor toward Hades's office.

In the daytime, the cafe was rather idyllic on the upper level. The scent of strong, sweet coffee and pastries filled the air, and the normally lush decor looked almost regal as the sun shone through the skylights. Not to mention it looked a hell of a lot less menacing when he wasn't terrified, naked, and surrounded by strangers or panicked pseudo-guardians.

While he had gone through the rest of his schedule—a history class on mythology that was supposed to be taught by Professor Leehan, but instead was being taught by his Painting instructor until Professor Leehan returned—he could not focus on anything except the unmistakable connection he felt to Izzy. Hades had called it a *hellfire* bond, and Spike hoped perhaps, his former Master would have some sort of insight on how best to navigate the shaky ground he felt he was on.

How did a hellfire bond differ from from what Cate and Gunner shared, or for that matter, what Hades and Darcy shared?

Or did Hades's origins mean he and Darcy shared a hellfire bond as well?

It was all rather confusing, but Spike knew one thing for certain.

Isabelle felt the same way he did, so why was she fighting him?

Why did things have to be so difficult, when they should have been much simpler?

Probably because you are a soul-reaping shifter who wants to bite her so you can break this stupid curse.

It was all he could think about during his mythology class—which hadn't actually divulged anything about mythology, despite *Calli's* ramblings about Gods and Goddesses and the impact they had on the modern day world.

If only she knew the truth, that Gods

and monsters walk among us, and they are oblivious to them.

Through her introduction, Calli did not disclose what had happened to his original professor, or why she was suddenly teaching another class of his. Thankfully, Isabelle was not there to distract him. Though Lorelai was in his class, she hadn't made a move to speak to him, and he had to surmise that was probably best. He could barely think straight as it was, and the last thing he wanted to do was slip up about what had happened between him and the vampire.

Does she know?

He wondered, being as the two women seemed close enough, but it was rather uncommon practice for a vampire to be gallivanting around with their primary source of food.

But Isabelle was not like the vampires he'd reaped long ago.

No, Isabelle was different, and perhaps she didn't see Lorelai the way most did.

Perhaps they really were truly just very good friends.

Hades opened the door to his office before Spike could even knock.

"How did you—"

"I have been expecting you," the tall, dark, and finely dressed man said ominously.

Spike pursed his lips as he walked in, casting his former Master a suspicious glance.

Hades closed the door as he motioned for Spike to take a seat.

"And perhaps I heard your footsteps

echoing in the halls, and no one dares interrupt me during my work hours."

Spike let out a small chuckle as he took a seat, leaning back in the leather chair.

"Except, Darcy, right?" he teased.

Hades narrowed his eyes as he straightened his tie. "I did not ask you here to discuss my personal affairs."

That's a yes.

Spike shook his head. "Of course, my apologies. I am feeling a bit... how do they say? Under the weather?" he asked.

Hades crossed his arms. "This wouldn't have anything to do with you staying up all night, causing trouble, would it?"

Spike could feel the corners of his lips turning up in a smile. The way Hades was standing, looming over him with that authoritative stare made him feel as if he was a child instead of a grown, twenty-one year old man.

A cursed man, but still a man.

"No, actually. I slept well, all things considered. I just... have a lot on my mind. Now, why am I here?" he asked, trying to shake the nerves that built within him under Hades's stare.

"Have you been intimate with her?" Hades asked, his voice stern and direct. The way in which he said the words were plain, as if they were no different than "pass the salt," or "have a good day, Sir."

Spike felt the blush creep on his cheeks as thoughts of his almost kiss filled his brain. Sadness and embarrassment threatened to erupt from his chest as he answered, "no."

He could not look at Hades as he

answered him, for he was embarrassed. Romancing a woman was just as difficult in this day and age as it had been when he'd lived as a human last.

Not that he'd had much luck romancing women in general when he was a soldier.

In fact, where romance was concerned, Spike's experience was rather limited.

Despite living in a time of record promiscuity, he'd kept his knot and his desires to himself.

After all, what woman would ever desire a man with his supernatural endowments?

He could not take that sort of rejection, and instead focused his attention on something he was better suited for.

Slaying monsters who were a threat to those he was tasked with protecting.

"I haven't um... you see, before I was cursed I, uh..."

Hades narrowed his eyes as he cocked his head to the side.

"Are you a..."

Spike felt like he wanted to crawl underneath Hades's desk and curl up into a ball and never leave. But fate was a cruel mistress, and though he wished with all his might he could shift at the moment, his hound was nowhere near the surface.

He sighed, hanging his head.

"It's not like I didn't *want* to, I just... hadn't met the right person, and I had people to protect under Athena's direction, and then I was cursed and..."

Spike looked up at Hades, expecting

to see judgment, disappointment. But instead he only saw understanding. Hades sighed.

"Athena's army? That's quite impressive," he said softly.

Spike swallowed harshly.

"Yeah, well, wasn't like I had a lot of options being what I am..."

"On the contrary, Spike. You are a rare breed, which means you are far more powerful than most shifters. I would think this sort of thing would be quite... enticing to most women."

Spike shrugged. "Yeah, well, it's not something I advertised, either. You know, on account of the—" Spike choked on his words, as he realized what he was about to say. The conversation had gotten away from him, and he needed to gain control again.

"The what?" Hades pressed.

Spike's heart raced, his body starting to heat from the panic. He'd never told anyone about his predicament.

"My knot."

Hades's eyes widened, but he only nodded as he hummed in understanding.

"So the other night, with this Izzy... What exactly happened then? Before your hound was baited?"

Spike leaned back in the chair, relishing its softness as it swallowed him and his woes, glad for the moment the conversation had steered away from his cock.

"We were dancing, and she just... she smelled so fucking good, and there was this energy between us, it was like... like the world was in slow motion and we were the only thing moving. And the way she looked at me, I thought... I mean, I might be a v-virgin, but I'm not completely inexperienced. I thought... I thought she was... on the same page... we almost kissed, but then... she... left," he said honestly.

Hades's eyebrows furrowed.

"I see," Hades said as he regarded Spike with steady gaze.

"Hellfire bonds burn faster than any other bond. Most bonds of fate run deep, and hellfire bonds are no different in that aspect, but the attraction, the sexual compatibility is much louder... upfront."

Spike blinked as memories of Isabelle filled his psyche. Of the heat he felt in her presence, or the fact that he couldn't stop thinking about her, or the overpowering *need* to touch her and possess her, from the inside out.

He looked away from Hades, his face heating like a flame.

"Hellfire bonds *need* to burn through this initial phase first. Once you've... mated, in the literal sense, the bond can solidify."

"So... once I have sex, it's all over?" Spike asked warily.

Hades shook his head. "No, Spike. Not by a long shot. Hellfire bonds are rooted deep. It's a bond that can't be broken."

Spike watched as Hades's eyes glazed, as his shoulders sunk. He knew that look all too well, for he'd seen it on his former Master's face for ages before he'd been given to Cate.

"But you broke your hellfire bond,

didn't you?" he asked.

Hades pursed his lips. "I did what I had to do to save Persephone's life. But it was not without its consequence."

Spike's shoulders fell. "But you still got your happy ever after in the end, right?"

Hades smiled softly as he nodded.

"Sometimes you have to go through hell to get heaven," he said, his voice somehow both commanding and empathetic. The silence between them was poignant.

"This Izzy, you think she is your mate," Hades spoke candidly, solidly. It was not a question, but a statement.

With Gunner and Cate, and even Darcy in the room, Spike had felt on display. But with Hades, his former Master, he felt at ease. He trusted the former God, and therefore he could not stop the words from falling out of his mouth.

"I know she is," he said quietly.

Hades pursed his lips, nodding in understanding.

"Then perhaps you better work on your... game. Do not try and rush the situation."

Spike cocked his head in confusion.

"How can you say that when you of all people know my time is limited..."

"That is precisely my point. You do not have time to waste shooting in the dark. What do you have to offer this woman, this *mate,* that she can not find in any mere mortal?"

Spike huffed in annoyance.

Way to kill a man's self-confidence, H.

"I do not mean to say you are not

without your qualities, Spike, but quite frankly, women desire more than just sex. Find out what she desires, what she *wishes* for. If she is indeed your mate, she will be just as starved for your heart as she is for the rest of you."

"Okay, well, this has been enlightening but—"

Hades smirked. "Indeed, it has. But I need to close up shop for the day. You can stay if you like, there will be a Speed Date tonight. Perhaps it could not hurt for you to observe other supernaturals, like yourself, in this environment. Perhaps, you could learn a thing or two about how the game is played."

Spike considered his words.

"I don't know if speed dating is my thing," he admitted.

"I hear Eve makes a killer sour apple

cocktail. Plus, I highly recommend the fried pickles," he said with a wink.

Spike smiled back, feeling a bit better as he headed for the door, stopping for a moment to turn and take in the sight of the tall ex-God, tucking his laptop into its case. He didn't look all that different from the Master he once had, but whereas Hades once emitted a vacuous energy of despair and pain, now he emitted a peaceful, warm energy that was hard not to respond to.

"Hades," Spike called, causing the debonair businessman to look up from his desk.

"Yes, Spike?"

Spike cast him a soft smile. "Thank you," he said as he exited his office, his stomach growling as he sauntered down the hallway.

SPIKE

Perhaps Hades was right, a drink and some food was exactly what he needed.

***

Hades wasn't kidding!

Spike took another long drink of his second sour apple martini, just as the buzzer sounded for a third time. He focused his gaze on the scene in front of him. Some of the faces looked familiar to him, but it had been so long since he'd seen any of them, and he knew they likely would not remember him. After all, most of them, save for Athena's brother, Mars, hadn't seen his face before.

Well, not his human face, that is.

"I don't know, man, I swear I get more action from the ladies over at the Den of Sin," Mars said as he pulled up a barstool nearby.

Spike wanted to say hello, and he almost did, except for the fact that Mars's sidekick, Pegasus, squeezed in the space between them, elbowing out Spike without a care.

His inner hound rose, instantly responding to what it perceived as a threat, and Spike couldn't deny the itch in his palm to show the stupid old winged shifter a thing or two.

He'd never liked the man even when he'd met him as a young soldier.

"I thought you were trying to turn over a new leaf," Pegasus irked his friend.

Mars scoffed. "Have you ever been to the Den and walked away with dry dick?" Mars did not wait for his proverbial wingman to continue before he announced, "I didn't think so."

SPIKE

Perhaps I should check out this den also... maybe I could learn from this den too.

But Spike did not have time to mull over Mars and the cocky horse's discussion, for the scent of roses and lilies wafted in from the outside like a fresh baked tray of cinnamon rolls.

Spike turned to see Isabelle arm in arm with her friend, Lorelai.

They both stood at the edge of the side entrance. Lorelai looked positively radiant in her white lace dress, her rustic red hair swept back to showcase her cherubic features. She looked as innocent as a rosy-cheeked angel, and even more so against Isabelle, who was wearing a slim, black satin slipdress that clung to her frame like a second skin. The sweetheart strapless neckline accentuated the curve of her breasts, lifting them so fully, he was half-certain if she moved just an inch to the left, she would have a wardrobe malfunction.

Which wouldn't be a bad thing.

His heart thudded in his chest, loud and clear as Hades's words reverberated in his brain.

Hellfire bonds need to burn through the sexual attraction first.

Is that what this was?

The haze of lust luring him to Isabelle because she was his mate?

What *did* he have to offer her besides his inexperience?

Besides his loud, racing heart, which knew in the depths of his soul, she was his end one way or another?

And as if the Gods themselves had sided with him for once, she turned in his direction, her gaze falling on him as a smirk graced her lips. She shook her head, whispering something in Lorelai's ear as they slowly made their way in, across the floor.

Lorelai whispered something back. Isabelle nodded in response. And with that, Lorelai left, and Spike took a sip of his martini. The tart apple taste burned his throat as he watched Isabelle make her way to the bar.

To him.

Fuck me.

"If I did not know any better, I'd say you were stalking me," she said, her voice edged in sarcasm.

Spike's insides burned like lava bubbling beneath the volcano.

"Maybe I am the one being stalked. After all, everywhere I seem to go, every chance I try to forget you... you just keep popping up."

"Why, thank you. I think that's the nicest thing any asshole has ever said to me," she said as she leaned against the bar. It was then that Spike noticed the seats were all taken, and so he stood.

Isabelle raised an eyebrow.

"It's yours," he murmured, not quite sure if he was talking entirely about the seat or...

Good Gods, what was in that martini?

Isabelle's eyes glowed with a fire that called his hound like a long lost dove.

"If you want it, I mean," he said, feeling the heat return.

Isabelle slithered past him, the motion brushing her legs against his as she elegantly sat in his warmed seat, crossing her long, fair legs.

The slit of her dress was high, and he could not help but trace the length of her skin with his gaze. He swallowed as he met her gaze.

"I didn't peg you for the speed dating type," he said.

Isabelle shrugged. "There's a lot of things you don't know about me, Spike."

"But I want to," he said without warning. It seemed as if every time he got near the vampire, he couldn't control himself. His speech, his touch, his desire.

Resistance was futile.

"Oh really, and what is it you want to know about me, hmm? My favorite color? My life history? Or perhaps you just want to know what I look like underneath this dress. Does that sum it up?"

Hades's words echoed in his brain.

Women desire more than just sex. Find out what she desires.

Spike felt strangely emboldened by the situation at hand, not to mention the sweet tart apple drink had relaxed him if only slightly.

Enough he could speak as candidly as Hades did.

"Perhaps we should start over," he said, licking his lips.

Isabelle narrowed her gaze.

"I'm Spike. I'm twenty-one years old. I'm a hellhound shifter who was cursed for the last couple centuries, and I've been human for less than a month, and I am very bad at this sort of thing."

"What sort of thing is that?" she purred.

"This," he said as he pointed back

and forth between them before gesturing to the room of speed daters. "The whole mating dance. And my favorite color is green."

Isabelle's lips pulled at the corners as he finished. She nodded at his drink.

"Is that what this is? A mating dance?" She casually slid her hand across the bar, tugging his drink toward her. He could only watch, frozen by her beauty and the tone of her sarcastic, sexy voice.

"It's only a dance if you accept," he said boldly. He watched as Isabelle's gaze softened, and just as she opened her mouth to speak, he saw a flash of red hair blur his vision.

"I'm bored," Lorelai said, crossing her arms.

Izzy's demeanor shifted entirely as

her eyebrows furrowed.

"Everything okay? You were gone awhile..." Izzy asked.

Lorelai shook her head. "I'm fine, just... this place isn't exactly as *lively* as I thought it would be based on all the reviews," she said. "I feel way too young to be here, everyone's like... in their thirties and forties." She wrinkled her nose.

"I might know a place we can check out," Spike said, looking between them. Izzy raised an eyebrow.

"Oh really?" She crossed her arms.

Spike nodded. "Yeah, Den of Sin. I hear it's pretty *lively*," he said with a grin.

Lorelai and Izzy exchanged looks as Lorelai pulled out her phone.

"It's like, twenty minutes away," she

said. "Uber can pick us up in two minutes," she said as she looked between Isabelle and Spike.

"Your call, Iz."

Isabelle looked at Spike, a wicked grin forming on her face.

"I accept," she purred, and Spike smiled in return.

Perhaps the night was just getting started...

CHAPTER TWELVE

IZZY STARED AT the line outside of Den of Sin. Spike was right, it *did* look rather lively compared the intimate, warm glow of the DeLux Cafe. The line to get in to the place was nearly wrapped around the building.

"How the hell are we even going to get in?" Loerlai asked as she tugged on her crossbody.

"I... didn't know it'd be this crowded,

I'm sorry, I—"

"Spike?" A woman's voice careened through the warm LA air, pulling their attention. Isabelle recognized the woman, even though she'd only seen her once before.

At the DeLux Cafe, with her... dog.

No, not dog... hellhound.

Spike...

The man who came with her, his arm draped around her shoulders, looked like he could take an army all on his own, his large biceps standing out against his tight tee-shirt. He chuckled as he nodded at Spike.

"Well, well, look who's out on a school night," he said as he licked his lips.

Isabelle watched the exchange warily.

Spike's eyes widened as his entire body tensed, his cheeks reddening.

"I, uh—"

The woman broke away from her muscle-bound man, reaching out to run her long black fignernails over Spike's arm, like she *owned* him.

The thought made Isabelle's blood *boil.*

Mine.

The word echoed in her brain. If looks could have started a fire, she would have set the woman's fingers ablaze.

"We need to talk," the woman said, as she tugged Spike away, pulling him aside.

Izzy stepped forward, but the large man only blocked her path. She stretched her neck to see the woman and Spike walking slowly, talking as if they were quite cozy. And she *hated* the sight.

"And you must be the lucky lady," the man said as he clicked his tongue.

"And who the hell are you?" Lorelai asked as she crossed her arms.

Isabelle kept her gaze on Spike and the nameless woman.

Just who is she to him?

An ex?

Isabelle knew she should not have cared about such things. After all, she had no claim on the hellhound who made her body hot like a raging fire.

Spike Moon did not belong to her in any sense of the word, but she couldn't help but shake the overwhelming need to *possess* this man, this shifter, as she watched him and the woman out of the corner of her eye.

"Consider me a... friend, of a friend of course." He smiled as Spike and the woman returned.

"Remember what I said," the woman spoke, her voice solid as she walked away, not bothering to look at the man she'd left with.

The man only shook his head as he regarded Spike. "Hey, Tony!" the man yelled, causing the concierge to shoot an angry look their way.

"Make sure my boy Spike and his lady friends here have a good time tonight, will ya?" he shouted.

Tony looked as if he wanted to murder the man, but thought better of it.

"Of course, *sir.* Will they be on your tab?" The venom in Tony's voice was not missed.

The man smiled. "Put it on Daddy Hades's tab, thanks."

Isabelle looked at Spike, who looked like he'd rather be anywhere in the world but in front of the Den of Sin with this man.

The man nodded at Spike as he walked past him, clapping him on the shoulder as he winked at him.

Tony raised an eyebrow at them. "Do make haste, *sir*, I haven't got all night," he gritted.

Spike shook his head as he looked at Izzy with a faint smile.

"Well, I think that's our cue," he said as he headed for the front of the line, toward Tony who was tapping his foot.

Isabelle followed, grinding her teeth, trying to quell the strange jealousy that seemed to be spreading though her body at the moment.

Her fangs ached to bite into Spike's

flesh, to mark him.

Then every woman, mortal or not would understand he was *hers.*

She swallowed harshly as she followed Spike, Lorelai on her tail as they entered the Den of Sin.

However illustrious and unassuming as it had looked from the outside, when they entered the main room, she soon realized they were all in for a rather *lively* night.

For the Den of Sin was not a bar or a club as they had been led to believe.

The servers were all dressed in various states of undress and leather, and while the lights shone over the room and bathed its patrons and inhabitants in shades of blue, purple, and red, she could see that there were plenty of couples—throuples as well—engaged in some compromising positions and situations. Not to mention there was a stage, where several people sat in small audience, watching a performance that looked like a woman being walked in leather, on a leash.

"I think I need a drink for this," Lorelai said shakily.

Isabelle turned to her, as Spike spoke.

"A drink would probably be a really good idea right about now," he said.

"I couldn't agree more," Isabelle said.

The three of them walked slowly to the bar as Isabelle took in the sights and sounds of everything around her.

"What can I get ya?" a petite woman dressed in a leather mini-dress pulled Isabelle's attention.

"Um... I'll just have a cherry vodka

and coke, thanks," she said.

"I'll have a water, thanks," Lorelai said with a deep sigh.

"You don't know how to make a sour apple martini, do you?" Spike asked curiously.

"Sugar, I can make you just about anything," she said with a wink.

Isabelle growled, the motion causing her lips to curl back and expose her fangs.

She knew it was dangerous to expose her weapons, especially in front of a mortal like Lorelai. Though if her friend noticed, she did not say anything.

She did seem rather... distracted since she'd come to the dorm, it had been her idea to 'get out and experience something new, something out of their comfort zones,' though it seemed perhaps her friend was presumptuous.

The night had gone well enough until Lorelai had suggested the cafe.

Where the tall, dark, and sinful looking shifter lay like the answer to her dark prayers.

And for a moment, it was like he truly was hers, the way he'd looked at her, the way he moved toward her so naturally... but the way the server was talking to Spike, the way she was looking at him, sparked Isabelle's hunger for blood in an entirely new way..

For this desire was less about needing to *feed*, and more about needing to protect what was rightfully *hers*.

Mine, mine, mine...

Isabelle knew it didn't make sense, but she couldn't deny the truth, either.

And the truth was that she'd never

felt for anyone the way she felt about Spike, and certainly not so soon.

"That will be all, *sugar,*" Isabelle said darkly.

The server shrugged as she headed off to fill their order.

"I will be right back," Lorelai said as she adjusted her dress.

"You sure?" Isabelle asked. "We just got here..."

Lorelai nodded. "I, uh... think I saw someone I might actually know, and I just want to say hi," she said as she looked everywhere but at Isabelle and Spike.

Isabelle noted she did seem rather distracted, and therefore did not think much of her behavior. Lorelai was quite the social butterfly. Isabelle nodded.

"I'm sure it'll be a minute for our

drinks anyway," she said.

Lorelai smiled as she headed off in the direction of the lounge, where rows of leather bound couches and VIP tables accented a small dance floor, which was quite dense with patrons.

It was just her and Spike, and the tension between them.

"Are you okay?" he asked as he leaned closer to her.

She hated that the movement alone made her entire body flush with heat. She turned away from him, watching the throngs of people around them touch, dance, and kiss as if they weren't in a room full of voyeurs.

The memory of the other night filled her brain. They'd danced together, under the moonlit sky at the party, and for a moment it seemed as if there was nothing else, no one else on the edge of the pool but them.

She'd wanted to kiss him, to wrap her arms around him and sink her fangs into his skin, to feel him all around her, possessing her from the inside out.

And such ferocity was terrifying, being as she'd never felt such feelings before in all her years of eternal life.

As she looked at Spike under the light of the Den, she couldn't deny she still felt the same way as she had the prior night.

Like she wanted to give in... but what was stopping her?

"I'm fine, " she nipped.

"You don't *seem* fine," he said as he cocked his head to the side, catching her wary gaze. "You seem like you're mad. Did I do something wrong? Is it because of this place, because honestly I didn't *know* it was a—"

"Who was she?" Isabelle asked, turning toward him, fire in her eyes.

"Who?" Spike asked, looking around them.

"The woman who pulled you aside?"

"Cate?" he asked, raising his eyebrows. "She's..." He paused as if he was considering his words very carefully.

"She's family," he said softly.

It was Isabelle's turn to look surprised.

"She... raised me. Sort of," Spike said as he ran a hand through his dark hair, his gaze soft and somewhat embarrassed.

"She doesn't look that much older than you," Isabelle quipped.

"Trust me, she's *much* older than she

looks," he said as he pursed his lips.

"What were you talking about?" she asked as she swayed back and forth on her legs, if only because she was worried if she did not move, she'd fall into Spike's proximity, and get all woozy again.

How was it this man was capable of puppeting her so?

"Nothing. She just... worries about me," he said as the server arrived with their drinks.

She glanced at Izzy and handed her her drink. "Enjoy," the server said briskly as she set Spike's drink down on the other side of the table, far away from Spike.

Good girl.

"But enough about... Cate," he said as he took a sip of his martini. "I'm really sorry if this place isn't your, uh... scene. I overheard some guys talking at the DeLux and I guess I just didn't want you to leave... again."

Isabelle stirred the ice in her drink as she contemplated her words.

"I have a confession, Spike," she said as she bit her lip.

"What is it?" he asked.

"I am not... good at this sort of thing, either," she said as she plucked the cherry from the tiny plastic sword in her drink.

Spike's lips pulled into a smirk. "And what might *this* be?" he asked.

Isabelle sighed.

Clearly I have lost my last marble.

"I'm still trying to figure that out," she said honestly.

"If it makes you feel any better... I've

never done anything like this before," he admitted.

"What? Gone to a sex club?" she teased. She didn't miss his blush.

"No, I certainly haven't done that, but what I meant was I... I've never done this," he said as he inched closer to her, his scent of fire and brimstone filling her lungs once more, making her entire body relax like jello.

Gods, he smells divine...

"I've never been on a date with a vampire before."

Isabelle smirked. "Well, I've never been to a sex club with a hellhound before." She took a sip of her drink, relishing in the crisp taste of cherry vodka.

"I mean, it wasn't what I was expecting, but..." She shrugged. "I like unpredictable and unexpected," she said with a giggle, as a man in a leather thong brushed past. "It breaks up the monotony of immortality. Makes me feel..."

"Human?" Spike asked, his lips pulling up into a delicious, sexy smile.

"I was going to say, alive. It makes me feel like I'm young again."

Spike took another sip of his drink.

"How old are you exactly?" he asked.

Isabelle let out a dark chuckle. "Rule number one of flirting Spike, you never ask a woman her age. Especially when she is immortal."

Spike held his hands up in mock defeat.

"I told you I was bad at this!" he said with a laugh of his own, his smile pulled back enough to showcase his pointed canines, and Isabelle couldn't deny the way the sight of them made her stomach flip.

She wondered momentarily what they would feel like, buried in her neck.

When she'd been turned, she already lay dying in the alley. The attack before the creature bit her was quite a painful, bloody attack. All the pain was channeled into her bones, her muscles, and the chill that ransacked her body as the blood drained from her veins.

Ricardo's bite had saved her life, but she'd never truly felt it in the way she suspected mortals did when they were bitten.

And though Isabelle had taken one-night stands over the ages, she'd never let a man near her throat. The implications were far too personal.

But the thought of letting this man—this hellhound—near her jugular made her body heat with flame, her legs press tighter together.

Spike lowered his hands as he grabbed his drink, regarding her with a look of understanding.

"It's not what I was expecting, either. But I guess with a name like *Den of Sin*, I should have known it would be..."

"Full of kinky fuckery?" Isabelle said as she raised her eyebrows, a grin spreading on her face. She couldn't help but laugh, given the situation.

"Yeah, I guess that about sums it up," Spike said.

"Well, when you're in Rome, you should do as the Romans do," she said as she held her glass up.

Spike looked at it before raising his

own. "When in Rome," he said as they toasted their glasses.

Isabelle watched him down the remainder of his drink as she sucked down the rest of her own in one gulp as the server passed her.

"I'll take another please," she bit.

Spike puckered his lips from the tartness of his drink, settling the glass down on the table in front of them as he nodded.

"I'll have another as well, please," he said politely.

The server smiled. "Coming right up," she said as she turned and headed for the bar.

Spike's golden eyes burned with interest as he looked back at Isabelle.

"Although, I feel like I should ask... what are the Romans doing this evening,

Izzy?"

Isabelle smiled wickedly as she nodded at the stage in the corner.

"Getting blitzed and living in the moment," she said as she sauntered over to the stage, giving Spike a rather tantalizing view of her backside. She did not have to turn and look to know he was following her, for she could feel his energy like a fire blazing after her.

Isabelle walked to the front row in front of the stage, her gaze settled on the sight before her.

The woman on stage was a rather attractive woman, her long dark hair pulled back in a braid and tied with a bright aqua ribbon that stood out against her tan skin and her demonic eyes. While most of the inhabitants of the den were in varied states of undress, the woman was practically naked save for a black harness that strategically covered her groin, black straps pulled tight underneath her breasts to accentuate the swell. Her nipples were visibly peaked, goosebumps evident amid her golden skin, and she was positioned on all fours. The man behind her had a leash wrapped around his wrist, the metal choke chain drawing a beeline to her slender neck.

Isabelle watched in awe as the woman was being choked, her leash pulled as the man behind her, a rather attractive looking demon with almost white blonde hair dressed in leather chaps, pulled the woman back into his lap with a rough tug.

"Be a good little pet and do as Master says," the man directed, his spit illuminated in the light from behind him.

But that wasn't what entranced Isabelle, though she couldn't deny the words or the way he said them was enticing. Her gaze settled on the collar around the woman's neck, which was bedazzled in red rubies and silver filigree. It reminded her of a much prettier version of Spike's studded collar, which he seemed to wear everywhere.

Izzy's gaze trailed over the forms in front of her, watching as the man's right hand pulled on the leash, while his left hand settled over the woman's breast, his fingers pinching her nipples as she rolled her head back against the man's shoulders.

Images filled her brain of Spike in the woman's place, naked on all fours, wearing nothing but a harness, long black straps tucked beneath his ass, around his...

"Holy hell," Spike's voice was barely a whisper, his breath warm on Isabelle's neck.

When had he gotten so close?

Isabelle swallowed as she blinked furiously, trying to put the images out of her mind.

The demonic man wrapped the leash around his wrist a little more, giving less leeway to his pet as he pulled her back against him. The woman arched her back as the man used his left hand to slide his arm up between the dip in her breasts, to her neck, his fingers sliding up and down the expanse of her chest, tugging at her nipples. The woman let out a soft *mewl*, like the sound of a contented kitten.

"It's... interesting, isn't it?" Isabelle said as a waitress walking by offered her a glass of champagne. She turned to look at Spike, noticing his pupils had dilated and he was already drinking half of his champagne.

"I'm not sure *interesting* is the word I'd choose," he said, his voice heavy with lust.

Something about the tone made Isabelle feel more relaxed. She couldn't help herself as she leaned back, falling against Spike while her eyes stayed glued to the scene in front of them.

The man walked his pet across the stage, stopping every so often to give her commands. When he stopped, the woman sat back on her heels, her eyes trained on her Master as he finally, slowly undid his leather chaps. Isabelle watched as they fell around his ankles, exposing his cock. His hand held the base, and she gasped as she laid eyes on something all too familiar.

A knot.

The sight caused a wetness to bloom between her thighs, a soft contented groan escaping her lips as her mouth went dry.

"It's…"

"Hot as hell," Isabelle murmured as heat ransacked her. She closed her eyes, taking a deep breath if only to try and regain control of the situation, of herself.

The memory of her last orgasm, fueled by thoughts of Spike and her KnottyDX5, filled her brain, causing her pussy to throb with need.

Spike's warm and intoxicating fire scent filled her airways, his body solid against hers. With her eyes closed, it was easy to pretend, to imagine Spike with a knot, erect and on display like the demon on the stage. Only, in her mind, Spike was the one waiting on his heels. Where she could take in the sight of him, pretty as a picture.

He set his hand on her hip, his palm sweaty against the fabric of her dress. And for a moment, it was as if they were right back where they started, on the edge of the pool at the party.

As the waitress came by with an empty tray, they discarded their glasses mindlessly, transfixed on what lay before them, and the fire building between them.

Without thinking, Isabelle snaked her arm up behind her, her fingertips brushing the edge of his metal spikes on his collar. The motion drew a deep groan from Spike, who burrowed his face into her palm, his lips brushing the heated skin there and causing a shiver to run down Isabelle's spine. Spike's cock twitched against her, causing a fresh wave of heat to overtake her as her knot-filled fantasies took flight, and she pushed herself back against Spike's hardness.

Fuck...

This is a bad idea.

Her eyes fluttered open again. It had been a long time since she'd been with anyone, let alone a man who made her feel as delicate as the relentless man behind her.

"Is that what you want, Izzy?" he whispered, his breath hot against the skin below her ear.

Isabelle's fangs ached, her throat going dry as she focused her gaze on the demon who now had his pet pinned to ground as he railed her from behind, pulling on her collar to make her look at him as he did so.

Spike's breath wavered as he spoke, the sound of his lust like a drug.

"No," she whispered as she tugged against one of the spikes on his collar, the motion drawing his lips against the flesh of her neck. The feel of his silky mouth against her skin caused her heart to beat faster, flared her thirst. And then Spike did the unthinkable as he kissed the tender flesh, as if he were afraid by doing so she'd disappear. As if she was more than just a pretty vampire he lusted for.

Spike kissed her neck softly, as if she

were a Goddess worthy of worship. Such a kiss as that, was bound to make Isabelle a goner.

"Oh, Spike..." she whispered, the desperation in her voice more than evident.

Spike slowly slid both his hands over Isabelle's hips, his shaky breath in her ear rocking her body like an earthquake.

"Tell me," he whispered, his voice full of so much emotion, so much desire. "Tell me what you want, and I will gladly will give it to you," he said the words like they were a prayer, a promise.

And she believed him, because his words struck a chord deep within her.

She was so hungry.

For blood, for lust.

For excitement, and the unknown.

For love.

For the man who made her feel like some weak, wanton little thing.

Like an animal in heat.

"I want..." The words were on the edge of her tongue, and she turned in his hold, the motion settling her front against his. She looked up into Spike's eyes, the fire in them as real as the one burning in her soul.

Perhaps it was the alcohol in her system.

Perhaps it was the rush and arousal of the show they'd been watching.

Perhaps it was the undeniable force she felt when she looked into Spike's eyes.

"I just want you," she said as she closed the space between them, taking Spike's mouth like the night takes the day.

Slowly, and then all at once.

Spike's lips moved against hers with fervor as she slid her hands up his chest. He let his trail over her hips, settling over her ass as he pulled her closer, his tongue caressing hers as a deep groan escaped him.

"Fuck, Izzy..." he murmured as he broke away. "You're going to make me shift..."

The desperation in his voice was like the rush of blood, and Izzy couldn't resist.

"Um, excuse me," the champagne woman was back.

Can't you see we're busy?

"Samael wanted me to disclose to you that there are vacant rooms which would perhaps be better suited for you," she said with a smile.

Spike blushed, and Izzy felt emboldened.

Her adrenaline was running, the alcohol was at its peak, and the last thing she wanted was to put a show on for wandering eyes. No, Isabelle wanted Spike all to herself.

"We'll take it," she said.

"Are you sure?" Spike asked, surprised.

Izzy watched his chest rise and fall with heavy breath as she licked her lips.

"I mean we don't have to—" he said the words, but Isabelle did not miss the edge, the hope in his voice as it caught in his throat.

"I'm sure," she said as she turned back to the attendant.

"Follow me," the woman said with a grin.

And as Isabelle grabbed Spike by the hand, leading him down a dark corridor, she had to admit she'd never felt so alive.

Because for the first time in her long, long life, she wasn't sure what to expect.

CHAPTER THIRTEEN

DESPITE HIS INEXPERIENCE, Spike had seen many things traveling in the shifter army in his youth. The Romans and the Gods and Goddesses they served were not without their depravity, their lust, and certainty not without their wild desires, and he was certainly not a stranger to voyeurism, as parties like that of the domina with the orgy of demons were not uncommon in his former life.

But something about the setting of the Den, the audience built in front of a stage while two demons put on a show, felt much more intimate. The sight alone was enticing, but it wasn't the woman on a leash or the man who ordered her around that made his cock throb and his inner hound salivate.

It was the sight of Isabelle before him, her eyes wide like saucers as she fixated on the performance, her signature lily and rose scent mixing with something much more potent. The sweet bite of arousal wafting off of her was just as intoxicating as any sour apple martini.

The rest of the world fell away as Isabelle leaned against him, as her body heated like a flame in his grasp. The sound of her sweet gasp and the way she arched her back against him, the cascade of her hair bristling against his tattooed arm, it was all too much. And as the world fell away around them, Spike felt his hound pushing him into the unknown, driving his corporal form toward the inevitable, and then Isabelle kissed him, and he knew there was no going back. For the taste of her on his tongue ignited a fire that would not cease, not until it caught along the edges of Isabelle's dress, her fingertips, her lips.

The animal inside of him wished to burn through the hellfire that existed in the dark space between them, needing her kiss, her touch.

Needing to bite her.

This is what I wanted, so why am I so nervous?

He wondered as he followed Isabelle and the waitress down a dark corridor. His inner beast paced with anticipation, his cock throbbing with the knowledge of what lay ahead.

But there was still a part of Spike that understood he was in over his head.

As bad as he wanted to mate with Isabelle—and he *did* want to mate with her—it all seemed to be happening rather quickly, at the speed of light. It was like he could barely breathe underneath all the sensations ransacking both his body and his brain.

The waitress punched in a code, opening the door for them. Inside, the light was red amongst the shadows, giving the room a rather dungeon-like appeal. He barely registered a word, his heart beating so loud in his chest he thought it would surely echo off of the walls. And then before he knew it, he was shrouded in the low, red light, the distinct thud of the door shutting behind him. Before he could speak, he felt Isabelle's hands on his chest, pushing him back against the cold, stone wall. Her lips crashed against his once more as the fire returned, as her hands traipsed over his chest, down his sides, over his...

A surprised sound escaped his throat as her hands settled over his hardness, causing his hound to rattle his cage once more.

The need to shift was pertinent, but so was the need to bite.

To sink his fangs into her flesh and taste her blood.

And so Spike fought back against her

hurried touch, pushing away from the wall as his own hands surveyed her body. Izzy's fingers hovered above his waistband. His hound growled from beneath his skin, the sound coming out of his own mouth echoing in the cavernous space.

'Slow down," he said, trying to catch his breath.

Isabelle looked at him with fire in her eyes, her irises rimmed with red coloring.

And Spike understood all too well what such a thing meant.

Somewhere in his psyche, he knew he should put an end to the moment. For dancing with a vampire while in bloodlust was quite a dangerous thing.

But as Isabelle unbuttoned the top of his jeans, as she rubbed herself against him, her lips trailing over his neck and jaw, Spike knew there was no turning back. Because her touch lit up every nerve in his body as his beast threatened to shift.

You need to burn through the attraction, first.

Hades's words danced in his head, and so Spike rationed there was no way out, but through.

He grabbed Isabelle's wrists in his hand, tightening his grip as she looked up at him with a gaze that was damn near crimson.

"I want—" Spike tried to blink away the red haze that fell over his own vision, unsure if it was due to the lighting of the room, or if perhaps it had to do with the vampire in front of him.

Words were quite difficult for him,

but the sight of Isabelle in front of him so hungry, echoing his own need, was all he needed to grasp the moment by the reins. He'd never felt such desire, such overwhelming need in all his life.

He had to have her, had to possess every part of her he could, and he needed to do it fast. For the shifting energy and his aching cock were starting to become damn near unbearable.

"What do you want, Spike?" Izzy said as she took a step back, biting her lip, the rise and fall of her chest fast and furious like the energy between them.

Spike sauntered toward her as his hound took hold, pushing him in the direction of his prey.

Izzy responded in tandem, taking an instinctual step back as he cornered her, until he'd backed her up against the chaise in the middle of the room. She fell against it easily, a sharp exhale leaving her as he stood over her, above her like the animal he truly was.

Never in all his life, as a man, a hound, a soldier, or a monster had he felt like a king, not in the way he felt when he towered over Isabelle, a fresh wave of her sweet arousal hitting him like fresh pie from the oven.

"I want to make you mine," he said, the words somehow in his voice, but not his own.

No, these words were his own, but the man he was in Isabelle's presence was new.

But he embraced it, nonetheless. He nudged her legs open before dropping to his knees, running his hands up her thighs, pushing her dress up. Her scent transfixed him as he ran his nose up her inner thigh, his hands pushing her back against the chaise. She smelled like heaven, and he felt like a demon.

Driven by hellfire and desire that was irrefutable.

Izzy leaned up on her elbows, her gaze fixed on him as he let his tongue taste her inner thigh. Sweat mixed with the sweetness of her arousal as he licked the evidence up, burying his face against the soaked barrier of fabric that blocked him from what it was he desired.

Spike's hands slipped in the sides of her panties as he pulled them down, but his strength was more than he'd anticipated. It was as if Isabelle's reaction, the *bond* between them, had given him more than he bargained for, and instead, he snapped the flimsy pair of panties clean off her body.

"Fucking hell, Spike..." she sighed, her voice heavy with lust. He continued to lick at her flesh, bathing her inner thighs in his warm saliva, trailing his way to her sex. His knot started to swell, his cock straining against his jeans as wetness bloomed at his tip.

"I'm burning up..." Her voice was full of heat, of desperation. "Make it stop," she whimpered.

His cock throbbed, aching for the warmth his tongue was lapping up like a delectable dessert. He palmed his cock, if only to settle the ache, but it did not help matters.

Izzy tightened her legs on the sides of his head, thrusting herself against his tongue as a deep groan escaped her. He watched as the hairs on her skin stood, as a welcome shiver escalated down through her, jolting his system as her legs spasmed, her fingers sliding through his hair as she gripped the locks tightly.

"Oh fuck," she cursed, her voice shrill. "I'm going to come," she said breathlessly, her words only exacerbating Spike's obsession.

Of all the things he'd tasted in his life, nothing tasted as sweet as his mate's wet, warm pussy.

More, more, more.

The hound inside of him wanted to feast. His hound wanted her body, her bloody heart, and her soul.

Isabelle's grip in his hair tightened as she thrust her hips forward, driving his tongue deeper, as if she needed *him,* as if she too, were starving.

He bit at her swollen clit, and Isabelle let out a bloodcurdling moan that he could have sworn shook the room like an earthquake. A deep growl escaped his throat as her pussy pulsed around his tongue, the sweet nectar-like juice of her release running down his chin. But he could not stop. He brushed her wet, trembling lips with his thumbs as he continued to lick, suck and bite.

Izzy moved, pulling his head up by his hair, regaling him with a glow in her eyes that was as equally beautiful as it was unsettling. In her gaze, he felt naked, seen for what he truly was.

A creature of hellfire.

Spike fell back on his heels as he gazed up at the vampire in front of him as she rose from the chaise, taking a step toward him. Frozen in her gaze, trapped, he felt an innate desire to please, to obey whatever this beautiful creature wished.

"You have no idea what you've done," she said, her fangs glinting in the light.

Spike's hound's hackles rose, recognizing the threat of the monster in their midst. But he could not bring himself to move, not unless it was what his *mate* wished.

"What I have done? It's you who has spelled me, *Isabelle*. It is you who have awakened the demon in me."

Izzy's red eyes glowed like rubies as she kneeled before him, meeting him where he waited. She grabbed him by his collar, pulling him close.

Spike's gaze held hers for a moment before she crushed her lips to his once more. He fell into Isabelle like a star from the sky as she pushed him down into the ground, her teeth nibbling at the flesh of his lower lip. She pushed him down by the chest, hurriedly finishing what she'd started moments before. A part of him was terrified as she all but ripped his jeans off, his anxieties surfacing as he hoped the sight of him—and his knot would not be overlooked.

That she would not run away as she had the night at the party.

For now that he had tasted Isabelle, he knew he'd never want anything else, anyone else ever again as long as he lived.

Live.

That was truly what Isabelle was, the gift of life, and he was nothing more than a curse of death.

But at the hands of this woman he

would die without her bite, and he certainly would die if she did not quell the ache in his soul that was staring to spread with every blessed moment that passed by in the dark, sinful dungeon of desire they'd holed up in.

"Oh my Gods," she said, holding her hand to her mouth.

Spike felt more vulnerable and on display ever than he had in his long life.

"I should have told you, I'm sorry, I—"

Isabelle's eyes glowed as she took his cock in her hands, her thumb brushing over the swollen knot, causing a jolt of fire to spread up his spine. Her touch was like velvet as she caressed his cock, her gaze locked on him, holding him in place. And just as Spike prepared for the rejection he feared, the unthinkable happened. Warmth enveloped him as

Isabelle sank herself down on his throbbing cock, the glide as he entered her smooth and wet.

Spike sat up, grabbing her hips as his hound and his human merged, dancing together in unison as instinct took over. He lunged forward, upending Isabelle back onto the ground with a thud, the overwhelming *need* to rut, to bite, to mark driving him, hijacking him.

Isabelle's back hit the ground with a smack, her fingers hooking beneath his collar as she pulled his lips to hers.

But her kiss was not what he needed.

His knot tingled with ferocity as he bottomed out, the sound of Isabelle's moan a most pleasant sound as he did so. Words escaped the booth of them as he thrust his hips against her, her warm, wet pussy clenching his cock *and* his knot like a vice.

And when he felt her walls pulse around him, when she *choked* him with all her might as she pulled his collar, her ecstasy ringing in the air, he could no longer see straight. He sank his fangs into her neck, and lost himself.

In Isabelle, in the hellfire, until the darkness consumed them both.

CHAPTER FOURTEEN

IZZY CRIED OUT in pain and ecstasy as Spike's fangs sank into her flesh. It wasn't an unpleasant experience, but in a way it was a splash of cold water to her system.

For as his throat swallowed down her blood, he instilled her with clarity.

Clarity that broke thorough the haze of lust.

Her innate desire to bite him was as

intense as the orgasm she was experiencing. But a bite from a vampire was a dangerous thing, considering the line between turning as Ricardo had done with her, and *bonding.*

Though Isabelle was uncertain the effects of her bite on a creature of hellish origin. Not much was known about the result of biting other supernaturals.

Would it hurt him?

Kill him even?

The thoughts ran rampant through Isabelle, igniting fires and anxiety all along the way, but even they were overpowered by the crash of pleasure as Spike's cock twitched inside of her, as his knot *popped,* the sensation better than anything she could have ever imagined.

All sense and logical thought ceased.

The heat within her had subsided, giving way to cold sweat. Her insides pulsed around him, and she could feel everything around her, converging all at once as he filled her with his release, as he drank her blood.

And all at once, reality hit her.

She'd let him *bite her*, drink *her* blood. She'd let him *in*. Into her heart, her body, her soul, and the most frightening reality was that she wanted *more*. For the first time she felt open, seen, and known, and that was more terrifying than any bite. Mixed with her own hunger, her thirst that was damn near devastating, she knew she was perilously close to giving in to a part of her she'd never known existed.

Spike collapsed against her, his fingers running down her forearm along her veins, and Isabelle quickly regained her strength. He slid out of her, and she did not miss the fruits of their coupling dripping freely down her thigh as she sat up, gasping for breath. Pain gave way to blissful pleasure as the world sharpened into view, her heart racing as her fangs ached to return the favor.

She pushed him away if only because the need to *bite* him was so prevalent, she worried she'd do it. And the moment his blood would hit her tongue—the moment she tasted its sweetness after so many years without—she was worried she wouldn't be able to stop, not now. Not when she felt so invincible. And the last thing Isabelle wanted was to hurt the man of her dreams. Because certainly Spike was the literal man she'd always dreamed of, tall, dark, handsome, attentive and sweet but yet full of fire, and capable of driving her over the cliff into ecstasy with or without his knot.

"Izzy, are you—"

"I have to go," she said as her cell phone chimed on the floor beside them. Glancing at Spike, she hated to see the pain, the rejection on his face. It cut through her like a sword, knowing she was the reason. But she needed air. She grabbed her phone like it was a life raft, capable of floating her back to dry land where there were no threats.

Around this insatiable man, she could barely breathe, and she needed to breathe.

She needed to process everything that had happened.

Where are you? I'm calling the Uber.

Izzy tapped out a response quickly.

On my way outside now.

"Isabelle," Spike's voice softened as he stepped toward her, but self-preservation had taken hold. No, she could not fall into this man like gravity, not now. For if she did, she knew it would all be over, for the both of them, and perhaps in some way she wanted to preserve the evening, not tarnish it with her anxiety, insecurity, and rampant hunger.

She set her phone down on the chaise, refusing to look at Spike, refusing to remember the sight of his sadness. Sadness she had caused. Tears threatened to rise up from within her, her voice cold a ice.

"It's Lorelai, I have to go, I—" She picked up the shreds of her panties as she cleaned herself up, before crumpling their remains and tossing them in the trash. Spike's eyes fell.

"I thought..." His shoulders loosened, his head hung in defeat. He ran a hand through his dark hair, pursing his lips.

"I'm sorry... I should go," he said as he dressed himself.

Isabelle did not wish to see him go at all, but she knew they could not stay.

How did this happen?

Isabelle ransacked her brain. Everything had happened so fast, it was like something or someone else had completely taken over her body and her mind.

As if some magical bond had formed in the blink of an eye and the thought of being without the maddening hellhound was a fate worth than death.

Yeah, maybe some distance is a good idea...

"I... I'll see you in class," she said, focusing on keeping her voice to sound as stable as possible, given the fact she felt as if she would break at any moment.

And with that, she ran out of the dungeon, leaving Spike alone, her heart breaking into pieces as she prayed she was doing the right thing.

***

The ride back to their dormitory was full of tension, neither woman wishing to talk about what had happened, despite their curiosities.

Lorelai seemed different. Though she hadn't seemed angry with Izzy that she'd lost her at the club, as Isabelle expected.

Instead, Lorelai seemed *relieved.*

She would have understood anger. After all, she herself was angry.

Angry that she'd let her whimsical desires lead her astray, down the corridor to the point of no return.

All of it—Spike, his touch, his kiss, his *knot*—all of it felt so undeniably right and perfect she had to wonder if she'd been dreaming. But the emptiness in her loins, the echo of his fangs in her neck told her it was far from a dream.

Isabelle played with her ponytail as she carefully covered up the sore spot on her neck where Spike had bitten her.

Only when the Uber had finally stopped, did she realize she hadn't spoken the entire ride.

"I don't know about you, Iz, but I'm fucking beat," Lorelai said as she slowly flashed her card at the front doors. It was quite late, due to the fact there was no RA watching the front doors. A part of her was surprised to hear her friend curse—the woman *never* cursed. She was a bright ray of sunshine and prided herself on her lack of foul language. So to hear her drop an expletive in such a nonchalant, careless fashion was something that would have alarmed Izzy had she been focused on anything except the throbbing site of Spike's bite or the ache in her fangs. Though the need for blood she often felt in the presence of mortals was nothing compared to the need to find her *mate* and sink her fangs into his skin. To make him *hers*. But she was tired, defeated. She was not herself.

Isabelle shrugged, feeling the

exhaustion like a blanket. She felt rather drained, both physically and mentally.

Lorelai unlocked their dormitory door, and Isabelle slowly ambled in toward their room.

Isabelle removed her dress, letting it fall to the floor. Lorelai turned the light on in their room for only a moment, and Isabelle could see her reflection in the mirror in the hallway. She stood for a moment, taking in the sight. She didn't look any different, but somehow she knew *everything* had changed.

The world around her and within her.

She was not the same Isabelle Constanza she had been before the semester had started.

She blinked away the tears that threatened to fall as she headed for the shower. The warm water on her skin should have made her feel better, but it only made her feel worse as she washed away the remains of the night's sins.

For the warm water and steam reminded her of the man who'd marked her; reminded her of his touch, his fire, and she could not help the tears that fell as she remembered the perfect, blissful moment he'd marked her.

She turned the water off, wrapping herself in a towel. As she traipsed down the hallway to the bedroom, she noted the soft snores coming from her mortal friend, who hadn't even made it out of her white dress. Lorelai's hair splayed around her like a ring of fire as she sprawled across her bed. She was always so put together, so perfect, it seemed out of character. But perhaps Izzy was not the only one undergoing a shift.

The light shone on her JoyBox, illuminating the swirl of blues and purples that were all too familiar. Isabelle stared at them for a moment before she kicked the box shut and shoved in with her foot behind the covers.

She crawled into bed, her skin damp from the recent shower, cold and in need of warmth.

Though as Isabelle pulled the covers over her naked form, she knew warmth would not come. Not from a flimsy comforter.

Her thoughts wandered to the man who intrigued her and terrified her.

To his amber eyes of fire, his sweet smile, and his silky dark hair.

His way with words, his penchant for

sour apple martinis. How he'd professed his desire to her, for her.

His promise that he'd do *anything* for her, that it was her who had somehow bewitched him.

It didn't make any sense, and Isabelle knew that.

You can't be falling in love with a man you just met!

This isn't a Disney movie, Iz!

As the words reverberated in her brain she knew it was pointless to argue with herself.

Especially because she knew now, after everything had happened, no amount of smoothing over would fix how she'd left things. Actions spoke louder than words, after all, and there was one thing Isabelle was quite good at— running.

A sole tear ran down her cheek as she forced her eyes close.

All she'd ever done was *run.*

Run from the monsters that chased her, the bloodlust that controlled her.

All she had ever wanted was something more than this immortal, lonely life.

And I just bit the hand that offered it all to me.

***

"I'm loving your use of lines in this, Lorelai, it's very expressive," Calli said brightly.

Isabelle stole a glance at Lorelai's painting, noting that it did look rather chaotic. In fact, Lorelai herself seemed to be unwinding a bit as the days went on. It was almost as if something had started the process of unraveling her tightly wound self.

"Thanks," Lorelai responded with excitement. "I just... have this sense of inspiration and I'm having a hard time keeping it bottled up, you know?" she said.

Isabelle's gaze focused on the man across the room, hunched over as he focused on his work.

She wished he'd look up for a moment, that he would catch her gaze as he had only days ago, when they'd serendipitously walked into the same class. But Spike did not look up from his painting. Isabelle's stomach growled, the hunger in her only intensifying.

"I sense a lot of turmoil in this one," Calli said, pulling Izzy from her daydreams.

"Oh, sorry, Calli, I—"

"A little turmoil can be a good thing, Isabelle. It is, after all, universal." Calli smiled softly as she stood next to her, regarding her with a knowing look.

"You would hardly be the first woman to record their qualms on canvas," Calli said with a light chuckle.

"I'm not—"

"It's all right, sweetheart. Your secret is safe with me," Calli said as she nudged her shoulder.

That was the moment she felt the fire, the steady burning at the base of where she'd been bitten. She turned in haste, catching familiar amber eyes of fire staring at her. Though Spike himself looked pained, his skin much paler than it usually did. A part of her wanted to rise, to go to him immediately. To tell him she was sorry, and soothe whatever had caused him such pain, though she knew the likeliest culprit was her. And she hated that.

"Before you all disperse today, I have an announcement," Calli called, driving everyone else's attention.

"The Leehan Gallery will be opening an exhibit on *magic*," she said as she clasped her hands together, a smile forming on her face.

"Specifically an exhibit that tells the story of magic during ancient civilizations, such as Greece, Rome, and more! It's going to be amazing, and I am so excited!" Calliope sighed.

"However, due to the size of this exhibit and the amount of artifacts as well as the renovations and preservation needed for these things, the gallery is looking for volunteers who can help catalog the artifacts as well as those who are handy with basic construction practices. If you are interested, this voluntary work can be claimed as extra credit and potential to move to a work-study position. It would look wonderful on a resume!" She said as everyone packed up their things. "If interested, please see me before you leave!"

Isabelle packed her things, as Lorelai hurried to do the same.

"Where's the fire, Lora?" she asked.

Lorelai blinked as she tugged on the strap of her messenger bag.

"Nowhere, but I told Calli I'd head over to the Gallery a bit early today to get a jump on the deliveries," she said. Something about the way she said the words felt off.

Almost as if she was lying.

But Lorelai never lied about anything, least of all to Isabelle.

Something is definitely off about her, and I plan on getting to the bottom of it.

"Okay, well, I guess I'll see you in a bit then, when I come in for my shift," she said, gauging her friend's reaction.

Lorelai nodded as she picked up her pace.

"Yeah, yeah, of course."

Isabelle set to leave, noticing Spike and Calli were talking. She'd known Calli from her exposure and constant appearance around the Gallery, and she didn't dislike the woman. In fact, she and Lorelai had seen Calli around the campus at multiple events, and the woman, always with a new man on her shoulder at every event, was always a source of excitement and inspiration.

But the sight of her speaking to Spike, how she ran her hand down his arm, caused Isabelle to see red. She knew she had no reason to be jealous or possessive of the man, especially considering all that had happened.

But all be damned, she was by their side in a flash, her fangs already pushing through as she nudged Calli aside.

This one's mine, Calli.

Back. Off.

"Isabelle! How perfect!" Calli said as she clapped her hands together.

"Spike, do you know Isabelle?" Calli asked.

Spike's amber eyes appraised Izzy, the rise and fall of his chest as his breathing caught more than evident.

"We've met, yes," he said.

The words were like a knife to Isabelle's soul. They were simple, emotionless.

It broke her heart.

"Oh good! Isabelle will be working at the Gallery today. She'd be more than happy to give you a tour of the place, get you set up. Isn't that right, Isabelle?" Calli's voice was sweet, full of happiness, and it took Isabelle a moment to understand.

She looked back at Spike, reaching her hand up to play with the hair she strategically covered her bite with. Though it had mostly healed, she still felt vulnerable displaying it. She wanted to keep such things to herself.

Wanted to keep what had happened between them to herself.

"Of course," she said, swallowing nervously.

Calli waved her hand. "I will catch up with both of you later, then."

Isabelle smiled, attempting to hide her panic from both the shifter who was making her blood heat, and her friend slash instructor who had decided to play matchmaker all of a sudden.

"I need a damn coffee," Isabelle mumbled, as she stared back at his endearing golden eyes. For a man dressed in all black with a collar and a badass skull tattoo, he looked rather... innocent.

"I am kind of hungry, actually," Spike said, flipping his dark hair out of his eyes. The sight made Isabelle's throat dry with thirst.

This was a very bad idea.

The worst.

"That makes two of us," she said as she headed for the door, Spike on her tail.

CHAPTER FIFTEEN

SPIKE FOLLOWED ISABELLE, who had taken off in a sprint.

It had only been two days. Two days since they'd gone to Den of Sin, since they'd given in to the hellfire bond.

Since he'd bitten her.

While he didn't regret what had happened, he knew that perhaps, somehow he'd crossed a line. He'd been so in tune with his hound, with the bond, not to mention the sounds and sensations he'd experienced while he and Isabelle…

A part of him wondered if he'd truly see her in class. She had been rather hurried when she'd left him at the Den, and he wasn't sure if given everything that had happened if she'd want to see him again at all.

Perhaps she regretted mating with him altogether, or perhaps she felt he simply was not very good at it.

Though he'd thought based upon the deep, pleasure-filled moans escaping her, he was doing *something* right, he also knew that an outward display was not always an honest one. He'd heard Darcy admit how often she'd faked her orgasms to Cate during their true crime-ice cream marathons.

Before she'd met Hades, that was.

The desire to hold Isabelle, to soothe her, and nurture the bite, the bond, was as bright as the feel of being buried inside of her. Spike lined up to cherish her, lick her wound, but she recoiled. She looked at him with a litany of emotion he could not understand, only moments after time and space had ceased.

But as soon as the bliss of their release came, it was over, and the truth was more than evident.

He'd bitten her. In the heat of things, driven by his animal, by fate, by his own heart's desire. He knew it would break his curse, but at the moment, he hadn't been thinking about such things.

The only thought he'd had was that he needed Isabelle, his mate.

He needed her to understand what was beyond comprehensible at the moment.

That he'd waited his entire life to be *hers* in every sense. As he held her, fit himself inside of her as he pushed her forward, he understood the magnitude of what that one word meant.

Mate.

Though it was true, he had no one to compare the experience to, but he garnered it would not have mattered if he had. Because the moment her insides clutched him, as she met his hurried thrusts, taking him knot and all...

He knew there would certainly never be anyone else, and his hound knew it too.

The instinct to bite overruled everything. The hellfire bond had burned, and in its place he was left with longing.

He wanted all of Isabelle.

He wanted to be *hers.*

And ever since, he'd been sick as a dog the last two days. Weak, tired. Starving, but unable to keep anything down. Until he'd found his way to class that morning, he'd considered calling Darcy. He knew hangovers rarely lasted days, but if anyone would know how to squash an impending cold or a broken heart, it would be the mortal. Cate, as kind and nurturing as she was, was not one to dote on the emotional or physical needs of people, and Hades was not any better.

And hell would freeze over first before he asked Gunner for *anything.*

"You okay, you look a little... pale,"

Izzy said as she opened the door to the library. The line at *Wake The Dead* didn't look particularly long. Perhaps they would have something to sate his starving appetite, and being as he felt a fraction better, he thought perhaps he'd be able to stomach a muffin at the very least.

It doesn't hurt to try...

An appetite that had reared its ugly head the moment Isabelle had entered his space. He stared back into her deep blue-green eyes, his blood heating, his heart skipping a beat.

Perhaps it is not food I hunger for...

"I am fine... just, a little tired is all. It's been... a long couple of days," he said honestly.

What else could he say?

"You ain't kidding," she said as they

walked to the end of the line.

"Listen, Izzy... about the other night..." he started to speak. The pertinent need to clear the air, to tell her the truth was overwhelming.

"Spike..."

"I'm sorry," he said as he stepped closer. Despite her tone, her scent and air soothed him. In her presence, he felt... better. Sated, almost.

Fate truly is a cruel mistress...

His gaze settled on her neck, the slightly pink marks that to the naked eye were barely noticeable, but to Spike's own eyesight, he'd see them even if he were blind.

His hound, his soul, knew its mark. The desire to comfort her, to run his tongue over her flesh was maddening.

"You..." She looked around before

whispering, "You *bit* me."

"I know, it just... sort of happened... I... "

"You're sorry? Do you even know what a... a bite like that means?" she asked in a hushed tone.

"Do you?" he asked, his eyebrows furrowing.

Isabelle's lips pursed into a thin line, her eyes of fire sparkling like the crest of the ocean, her gaze just as dark and deep.

"I know shifters do not bite to turn, they bite to... to bond."

Spike hung his head.

"I'm sorry, Izzy. I should have told you, I should have asked before—"

"What can I get you?" the cashier drawled, looking nonplussed.

"I'll have a Edward, please," Isabelle

said tightly before glancing at Spike.

Suddenly his appetite for muffins diminished.

I really fucked things up, haven't I?

"Don't think I don't know what you're doing," she said as they moved up an inch to the right as Isabelle slid her card back in her pocket. Her voice was quite matter of fact.

Spike raised his eyebrow.

"What I am doing?" he asked in confusion. "I don't understand, what is it you think I am—"

"Driving me insane," she said as they moved up.

"Me? Driving *you* insane?" he said as she held up her hand.

"Don't do that," she said.

"Do what?" he asked, confused.

"You can't just... you can't just give

me multiple fucking o's and then be all cute and sorry, and make me feel so fucking flustered!" she said as she kicked the front of the counter. The baristas didn't even blink.

Multiple o's...

"You drive me batty, Spike Moon. You show up on campus, cause my fangs to ache, my damn blood to heat..."

She threw her hands up in the air. "You have no self preservation. Don't you know *what* I am?" she crossed her arm.

"Of course, I do, I—"

"Then why do you pursue me like I am nothing more than, than—"

"Edward," the barista yelled, breaking up the moment.

Izzy snatched the cup up, brushing past Spike. The touch, as minimal as it was, caused a jolt of electricity to run through him.

He followed her without question as she sucked down the liquid, heading past the library doors.

"I know what you are, but I don't *care* about that," he said honestly.

Isabelle shot him a worried glance.

"You should," she warned. "I could end you," she said solidly.

"But you didn't. You haven't and I don't think you would if given the chance because..."

They stopped just outside the doors to the gallery. Spike sighed as he gazed down at the beautiful creature before him, the words falling out of his mouth without warning.

"What have you done to me?" she whined as she stared back at him.

"You have turned me into some...

some... lovesick creature I don't even recognize," she said quietly.

She pushed the door open, breaking his gaze. "But I guess none of that matters, because we have work to do," she said as she walked through the door, and all he could do was follow.

***

Spike unpacked the third box in an hour, setting out the rocks and talismans that were strategically packed in velvet lined boxes. Izzy sat on the opposite side, placing the varied objects into their rightly sized cases that would be on display for the show the following week.

His hand wrapped around something without a box, a loose stone that was smooth, like obsidian, but as he pulled it out he could see it wasn't dark by any means. It shimmered like a diamond, its smooth undertones catching the low light as a faint humming sound emanated from it.

Spike's entire body tensed as power radiated through him, rattling him and making his stomach flip.

The stone emitted a low, teal light, fractals of energy racing out of it across the canyon between him and the woman of his dreams.

His mate.

And all at once Spike knew he'd set his hand on a most precious artifact.

A diviner.

He needed to call Hades immediately, but he was transfixed for the moment not on the stone itself, but the lines between him and Isabelle. They were faint, flickering.

As if perhaps the bond he felt was not as strong as it felt in his heart.

Because it is one sided, he realized.

Isabelle looked up, nonplussed by the sight in front of him.

"You don't see it, do you?" he asked, his voice dropping an octave.

Izzy cocked her head to the side. "See what" she asked.

Spike closed his hand around the stone as he handed it to her.

"Nothing," he said as he forced a smile. "Let's get this box finished."

CHAPTER SIXTEEN

SPIKE SAT IN Hades and Darcy's living room, sweat starting to form a sheen underneath his black v-neck.

"And you are certain it was a diviner?" Hades asked.

"I'm more than positive. It looked just like the one in Hell's Archives," he said as Hades crossed his arms.

"And you have access to this Leehan Gallery, where it is being kept?"

Spike nodded as he held up his campus ID.

"Calli got it registered this evening before I left."

Cate shook her head. "I thought... I thought the diviner from the archives was recovered."

Hades pursed his lips, a deep sigh leaving him.

"Well... actually—" Hades ground his teeth. "Orion had it last."

"Oh for fuck's sake!" Cate snapped.

"Wasn't he technically working for you... you know, like while you were gone..." Darcy asked.

Hades shrugged. "Technically... it wasn't supposed to be there in the first place... and Lucifer wasn't all that keen on returning it... so..."

"You mean neither you nor the Archer

kept track of it and the big guy downstairs didn't ask questions, so you two had *no fucking idea* where it ended up," Gunner nipped.

Spike's breath hitched as a fresh wave of nausea rolled in.

"In the grand scheme of things, *Gunner*, it did not matter. It isn't a weapon, it's a tool of divination, a tool of fate," Hades answered. "It doesn't *hurt* people. It only shows them the truth."

"Spike, are you feeling all right? You look a little heated..." Darcy said as she sauntered over to where he sat.

"I'm just hot, I think... I think I'm coming down with one of those awful human flus or something," he said as he removed his shirt.

Darcy used the back of her wrist to feel his head, the temperature difference startling even to him.

"You're burning up, Spike," she said with concern.

"Maybe it's the curse," Gunner said ominously.

"What?" Cate turned, her eyes frantic. "He's got weeks, he—"

"You didn't bite anyone, did you?" Gunner asked more seriously. "Like one of your lady friends..."

Spike's throat had started to go dry as Gunner's words fell on him.

"I... did," he admitted.

A round of cursing whistled in the air around them.

"Isabelle?" Hades asked as he came to stand by Spike.

"Yes," Spike admitted as his hound started to pace, to push against his insides. His stomach rolled with another wave of nausea.

"I don't feel so good," he admitted as he braced himself on the couch. Darcy and Cate flocked to him, sitting beside him.

"Is that... like, can that make you sick or something?" Darcy asked, worried.

"Not usually..." Cate said. "I mean, shifters bite to bond, not to kill. They don't have venom or anything like a vampire."

Spike felt as if he were truly going to expire. The heat mixed with the nausea as reality dawned on him was too much.

Venom.

Vampires have venom...meant to paralyze their prey, so they could feast on their blood.

He hadn't thought twice about

sinking his fangs into Isabelle.

He'd known what she was, and she had tried to warn him... hadn't she?

He'd been so concerned about breaking the curse, he hadn't thought about the sliver of a chance that perhaps it would *not* work.

Or it could backfire...

"Vampire venom..." he said, his voice faraway as he struggled to comprehend it all.

"Isabelle..." Hades said, his voice solid and unwavering. "She's mortal, right?"

Spike shook his head slowly.

"No," he said as he closed his eyes.

Cate ran her hand up and down his back.

"She's a vampire," Darcy said, the worry in her voice evident.

Spike nodded.

"This is worse than I thought," Hades said.

"I think... I think I need to lie down," Spike said as he leaned his head on Cate's shoulder.

"Don't worry, Spike, we'll fix this, I promise," she said, her voice the last thing he heard before darkness overcame him.

***

"You bit me." Isabelle's voice was soft, hazy.

She sat across from him, dressed in her black dress, the one she wore the night they'd gone to the den. Where he'd bitten her...

He was so sure it would have broken the curse...

"He doesn't seem to have any similar markings," Gunner said, his voice tinged with pain.

"That means she didn't..." Darcy's voice was soft.

"But without her bite, he'll..."

"Die," Cate whispered.

Die?

When was death an option?

"The venom in his blood needs to synthesize. It can't do so without a reciprocated bite." The far away voices of the Fates echoed in the space around him.

Where am I?

Where is Hades...

I don't hear his voice...

"Do we know anything actually helpful?" Gunner asked.

Spike could have sworn he sounded...

sad, disappointed even.

Like he *cared* what happened to him...

"His body's been fighting it for days at this point. Without a bite from the source of the venom, I'd give him maybe forty-eight hours," the fate said.

Forty-eight hours...

But I just got here...

Spike's hound whimpered, his heart broke.

He'd spent such little time as a human before he'd been cursed, and in the past month, he'd only started to scratch the surface on the vibrant, chaotic world he'd awakened in... awakened by his mate.

I'm sorry... Isabelle said as she crawled closer.

I told you I was dangerous... you

shouldn't want me...

"But I do. Not because I believed you could break my curse... but because... it was fate," he said as he ran his fingertips along her soft, chilled skin.

"I don't believe in fate," Isabelle said as she straddled his lap.

Spike ran his fingers up her spine, relishing in the softness of the fabric against his fingertips.

"I do. I believe you were meant to find me, to bring me to life."

Isabelle trailed his fingers down his cheek to his neck, toying with the spikes on his collar.

"I bring you nothing but pain," she said, a sole tear running down her cheek.

"You bring me bliss. You open my heart and you free my soul." He leaned in and kissed her, her lips soft and sweet. It

almost felt... real.

"All I am, all I ever was... was yours. I know that now."

"I don't want to hurt you," she whispered, tracing her fingertips along his face. "Or worse, I don't want to be the reason your soul disappears..."

"A kiss and a bite of death," he murmured into her hair as the world around them dissipated, a gentle hand shaking him.

"You can't hurt me. You saved me. My soul is yours to take, Isabelle. I knew it the moment I saw you. I am yours, and I will always be yours," he said as he kissed her tear-stained cheek.

"Spike..." her voice faded into the darkness.

A gentle hand shook him, pulling him from his dreams.

"Wake up, Spike. Someone's here to see you," Darcy whispered softly.

CHAPTER SEVENTEEN

IZZY FELT A pang in her chest that radiated outward.

"Fuck!" she said as she tried to catch her breath. It had been nearly three days that Spike had been absent from class, and he hadn't shown up to the Gallery, either. Though Isabelle didn't want to believe her periodic chest pains and the shifter's absence were related, she knew better. It was either bad luck or serendipity.

"All this time with the mortals is rubbing off on you, I see," Eric said as he strung lights from one corner of the room to the other.

"I really appreciate your help on short notice, but I could do without your judgment," Isabelle said as she rubbed her chest. The pain ebbed beneath her skin, her body inflamed like a literal burn.

She swallowed harshly. Her throat was dry, and she was quite hungry. Though her appetite was for one thing, and one thing only.

She'd walked past mortals without blinking, unphased by the endless swell of blood at her disposal. Where she used to fear large crowds because she thought she'd be tempted, mortals tempted her no more.

She longed to taste the sweetness of hellhound shifter blood.

Spike's blood.

"Lorelai, can you hand me a hammer, please," Eric called out.

Lorelai shook her head, breaking out of her daydreams. She seemed to be much more distracted as of late.

Perhaps I am not the only one who's losing their marbles...

"Sorry, I, uh... hold on..." she said as she left the room in search of the tool.

"Where's your handsome friend? Striker... was it?"

"Spike, you mean?" Isabelle asked.

Eric nodded. "That's it."

"You want the short version or the long version?" she asked with a sigh as she rubbed her chest.

Eric pouted his lips, considering her words.

"Hmmm, I'll take 'Is it complicated' for five hundred, Alex."

Isabelle scoffed.

"Complicated doesn't even begin to cover things..."

Lorelai came back with the hammer, looking between them.

"What? Did I miss something?" she asked.

Eric and Isabelle exchanged a glance.

"I was just getting the scoop from Izzy about her new beau..."

Isabelle rifled through the collection of rocks and crystals, readying to set them in their prospective cases as she sighed.

"He is *not* my beau," she bit, though the words themselves tasted wrong. Her defensiveness was sour to her own ears, and she regretted their truth. Spike was not *hers*. She'd made damn clear to him he wasn't anything of the sort, albeit because she was scared of what such a thing meant.

Isabelle had been alone for far too long to remember how to be... anyone's anything.

One passionate tryst did not make a love match, sex was just a part of the bloodlust equation, wasn't it?

She sighed as Lorelai raised a brow at her.

"Oh, this should be good..." Lorelai chuckled.

"The short version, then," Izzy deadpanned. "Put simply... boy meets girl, girl is intrigued, boy kissed girl, girl doesn't want to hurt to boy, girl and boy have *amazing* sex, boy bites girl…"

"Bites?" Lorelai asked, her voice rising with surprise as Eric chimed in equally surprised with, "Holy hell…"

Isabelle shrugged. "I mean, it's not that *shocking*…" she said with a blush.

Eric let out a dark chuckle. "Well, some of us thought you'd gone celibate, so it's nice to know we were wrong," Eric laughed.

Isabelle pointedly flipped him off.

"Fuck you, Eric!"

He only let out a deep laugh, and Lorelai chuckled as well.

"Never thought I'd see the day you let someone *bite* you," he said with a whistle. "Given the circumstances, and all."

"Circumstances?" Lorelai looked between them.

"She doesn't know?" Eric asked inquisitively.

Panic flooded Isabelle at his words.

"Know what?" Lorelai asked.

"Isabelle and I are vampires, darling. Surely you don't think *these...*" he said as he exposed his fangs, "are just for fashion," he said as he handed her back the hammer, moving the ladder down to the next set of walls.

To her surprise, Lorelai did not flinch or falter.

In fact, she seemed almost jaded at the reveal.

How anticlimactic.

Lorelai twirled the hammer in her hand. "I mean, Gods and Goddesses exist, so why wouldn't vampires?" She shrugged.

It was Isabelle's turn to be surprised.

"How—"

"I'll fill you in later," Lorelai said with a smirk, leaving Isabelle stunned.

Eric only laughed. "We may need to keep you around, Lorelai. I don't think anyone's been able to shut her up like this in the history of forever."

Lorelai giggled.

I have fallen into the literal Twilight zone.

Last marble has left the building.

"As I was saying..." Isabelle scoffed as the laughter died down.

"I'm sorry, please continue," Eric said, smirking mischievously.

"It's not just any bite, I'm afraid, it's..." She paused, trying to find the words.

For once she said them out loud, she knew it was over. There was no hiding, no pretending it didn't happen. Spike had *bitten* her. While she hadn't much knowledge or experience directly with other supernaturals like herself, some things were the same no matter what.

Biting someone was done to either turn them or bond them.

Both life sentences.

Her voice wavered as she realized Eric and Lorelai were looking at her strangely, their faces cast in blue light.

Funny, I don't remember the fairy lights being blue...

"Iz, why is your rock glowing?" Lorelai asked warily.

Isabelle looked down, gasping as she noticed her friend was right. The smooth, shiny rock in her hand *glowed* brightly, a faint hum emanating from it. But the light that came from it was a ribbon of energy, drawing curved fractals from her chest to the rock and out the door...

"I think the creepy rock wants you to follow it," Eric said with excitement.

"That sounds like a terrible idea," Izzy said as another pain shot through her chest, this one nearly knocking her over.

"Fuck!" she cried out, dropping the rock, and the lights went out.

"Izzy!" Lorelai's soft voice changed to one of panic as Isabelle felt her friend's touch on her arm.

"Are you two okay?" Eric asked, his voice stable and unwavering, despite the darkness.

"I've been getting these awful chest pains all freaking evening..." she said as she sucked in a breath. "I think it's..."

"Because of the bite?" Lorelai asked

as the lights flickered before dying out completely. The fairy lights, the overhead lights, all of them. The room was shrouded in darkness, the only light source the bright, whitish blue of the rock and its ribbon like energies, lighting her way through the exhibit, out the door...

Isabelle rationalized nothing good ever came from magical artifacts, but something in her heart, in the pain that emanated through her being, told her there were forces far beyond what she could even begin to comprehend, forces that were pushing her in the direction of fate.

"The bite... the rock... the pain in my chest..." she said as she caught her breath. "It's all too much to be coincidence."

She had no idea what lay on the other end of the rock's glowing lines, but she had an inkling of what she thought it would be, or rather *who.*

Her fangs ached, and her stomach tied in knots.

"Well, what are you waiting for, Iz? Follow the blue rock road!" Eric said as he and Lorelai huddled around her.

"And what if I don't like what we find?" she asked, uncertainty threatening her sanity.

What if Spike wants nothing to do with me?

I've pushed him away time and time again...

"Isn't that the point of a diviner?" Eric asked, pulling her attention.

"A diviner?" Isabelle asked, feeling a wave of nausea.

"I've actually heard about this," Lorelai said as she reached out to touch the rock.

"It was covered in class the other day. The Gods used them to divine true love matches for the humans and themselves…"

'Of course they did," Isabelle said dryly as she set forth toward the doors.

"Oh, so chances are your new boy toy is on the other end of that rainbow then," Eric said gleefully.

"Only way to find out," Isabelle said as she followed the light, a dark pit forming in her stomach.

If Spike truly was on the other end of the magical lines, why did she feel so afraid?

Why did she feel like she was headed straight for the depths of hell?

Isabelle closed her hand around the rock, if only to keep her gaze in front of her, paying attention to her surroundings. Though it seemed as if every step, the lights continued to go out, almost as if the energy of the diviner was draining everything around her or something...

"Are you Isabelle?" A dark voice emanated from the shadows, stopping Isabelle and her friends dead in their tracks. The low, flickering library lights ominously added to the eerie moment, and that was when Isabelle saw him.

He didn't exude a supernatural air as Spike had, but there was some sort of resemblance. The sharp-dressed man had dark hair and eyes, like Spike, but he looked much older, much more refined in his black suit and tie.

Is that Spike's...

"Who's asking?" Eric said as he bared his fangs, stepping in front of Isabelle and Lorelai.

The man only raised an eyebrow, nonplussed at Eric's display of dominance.

"Honestly, of all the colleges, he picks one riddled with vampires," the man said with disdain.

"I'm not a vampire!" Lorelai said with a growl.

"Then that must make you the lucky one," the man said as he stepped forward.

Eric hissed.

Isabelle pushed him aside.

The dark-haired man nodded to the light emanating from her fingers.

"That does not belong to you," he said

simply.

"Who are you?" Isabelle asked, her voice solid and unwavering.

The man smirked.

"I am Hades," he said smoothly. "And I believe we have a mutual friend who is in need of your help."

"My help?" Isabelle said, her voice small.

Hades nodded.

"Hades... like... God of the Underworld, Hades?" Lorelai chirped.

"I have moved on from the Underworld, but yes."

"Holy hell..." Eric said with another whistle. "This day just keeps getting weirder and weirder..."

"Daddy Hades..." Isabelle murmured as her memory took hold.

Put it on Daddy Hades's tab, the man

at the Den said, before he'd left Spike and her alone...

"Shit, you got that right..." Eric bit.

"Are you Spike's dad?" Isabelle bluntly asked, steamrolling over Eric's comment.

Hades threw his head back with a laugh.

"No," he said plainly as he motioned to the doors. "But I have cared for Spike likely longer than you have been alive, which is why I am here, to find *you* to make right what you have done."

Isabelle felt a stabbing pain in her chest. She cried out as her knees buckled and sweat started to form on her brow.

"No offense, Hades... sir... but, uh... we're kind of on a mission to find—"

"Oh fuck, it hurts!" Isabelle gritted,

dropping the diviner as her hand clutched at her chest.

Lorelai kneeled beside her.

"It's worse than the last one..." Isabelle said as she fought to regain her breath.

Hades knelt smoothly as he picked up the rock, turning it in his fingers.

"It appears, Spike is not the only one in danger," he said. "We must not waste time. You need to come with me,"

"Are you fucking crazy? How do we know you won't, like, put us six feet under?" Eric snapped as Hades advanced on them.

"I'm afraid if you want to help your vampire friend here, you don't have much of a choice."

CHAPTER EIGHTEEN

ISABELLE WOULD HAVE been more impressed with the sleek, black sports car that Hades drove had she not been so feverish.

She wasn't completely certain she wasn't, in fact, dying.

This is the price I pay for letting a hot hellhound fucking bite me...

"How are you feeling?" Lorelai asked as she ran her hands through Isabelle's hair while Eric and Hades fought over the music playing on the radio.

"Shotgun always calls music, that's the rules! Everyone knows that!" Eric nipped.

Hades glared at him before focusing back on the road.

Isabelle couldn't make out where they were, due to the heavily tinted windows, but she knew wherever they'd gone, *he* was close. She could feel him, the connection a faint echo in her blood, in her bones. But even without the energy, she knew because the diviner in her palm vibrated like her bullet, rattling against her heated palm with urgency.

"Like I've been bitten by a damn hellhound," she mused. "And I'm headed straight for hell."

"You aren't actually taking us to hell,

are you?" Eric asked.

Hades scoffed. "I told you, that part of my life is in the past. I am much more interested in the preservation of life these days than that of ending it."

"So what's the plan?" Isabelle asked as she forced herself up to roll the window down. The chill of the air was welcome to the heat she was experiencing.

"Isabelle," Hades evaded Eric's questioning as his eyes stared back at her via the rear view mirror.

"What?' she asked as she sucked in a fresh, clean breath of air. Wherever they were going was out of the city, as there didn't appear to be a high rise in sight. Instead, all she could make out was the dark shape of trees and brush, and the moon that hung in the dark sky.

"We will be arriving soon. I need you to tell me what happened, in your own words before we ascend the main driveway."

"What do you mean, my own words?" she asked, her eyelashes fluttering.

The heat was practically unbearable between the fire in her blood and the vibrating diviner that glowed in her hand.

Eric turned to look at her. "How did it happen, Iz? The bite?"

Isabelle wanted to crawl into a corner and never come out. The last thing she wanted was to share her experience—the details of their lust-driven fuck—with a man she saw as her brother and Spike's Dad-Not-Dad.

But if it means finding a way through this insanity for the both of us...

"It all happened pretty fast," she said as she shifted in her seat uncomfortably.

"You know how it goes... one thing led to another and—" She swallowed.

"I knew what was happening, I just... didn't have time to process it. I was so fucking hungry, and so fucking close—"

Heat radiated from her being as she realized she'd said too much.

Maybe death is a better option.

"You did not bite him?" Hades asked.

Isabelle felt exhaustion take hold. Sleep sounded like a really good idea.

"No," she said softly. "I didn't want to hurt him," she whispered.

"That has to be it, then," Hades said as he picked up his phone.

Isabelle laid her head back on the seat as she let the wind kiss her face.

"Wake him up, we will be there in less

than ten minutes," Hades barked to someone on the phone.

"I think I'm just going to shut my eyes," Isabelle murmured, as darkness overtook her.

***

"Iz, wake up. We're here," Lorelai said softly as she shook her.

Isabelle blinked, her limbs feeling like dead weight. Her body was still hot, and she felt rather sweaty from the humidity amidst her own fever.

"You need to get up," Eric said as he slipped his arm behind her, pulling her out of Lorelai's lap.

As she stood and her sight adjusted, she had to take a moment to remember to breathe.

For the *house* in front of her looked

like something out of an architectural magazine. But it wasn't the oversized windows or the metal framework that awed her, no.

It was the glowing blue ribbons that led from beneath her fingertips through the windows to...

Spike.

Isabelle took a slow step forward, then another, and another, until she was on the precipice of the property, her body moving of its own accord. Her hand trembled as her entire body *ached* for relief as she reached for the door handle.

She knew relief lay on the other side of the door.

She reached her hand out, all noise and sensation around her dissipating as the click of the handle sounded loudly in her ear.

She was vaguely aware that Eric, Lorelai, and Hades were behind her, but she didn't care.

Her heart thudded in her chest louder with every step as she pushed forth into the unknown.

"Clear the room," Hades ordered, and it was then that Isabelle realized there were more people. Watching her with intensity. She even saw the woman and man from the club, Cate and… the man who called Hades 'Daddy'.

"Hades—" Cate protested. "We don't know if—"

"I don't often agree with H over here, sweet cheeks, but trust me when I say it's for the best," the man said as he tugged her hand down the steps.

"What if it doesn't work, what if—"

That was when she saw *him.*

Standing at the edge of the steps, looking paler than an actual vampire. But his eyes still held that effervescent golden glow that she couldn't resist.

And all at once the world fell away, and Isabelle knew.

No matter how hard she'd fought fate, it still brought her here, into this ominous house, with friends and strangers surrounding her. It still brought her out of the darkness and into the light.

"Isabelle, how did you—"

Isabelle took one stop forward, then another, until she was on the landing of the stairs.

"I, um... you haven't been in class," she said, chastising herself for her inability to synthesize words.

But perhaps words were not what she

needed.

Spike gripped the edge of the doorframe, his knuckles going white. His dark gaze held hers as she stepped up on the top stair, the motion putting her almost flush against him. Sweat covered his pale, shirtless chest, and he smelled like fire, brimstone, and something else... something she hadn't understood until that moment in time, where his gaze captivated her.

He smelled like *mate*.

"Can we..." She sucked in a deep breath as reality overwhelmed her.

"Can we talk?" she asked.

Spike nodded as he stepped away from the doorframe, reaching his hand out to trail his fingertips along her cheek.

A jolt of energy—no *fire*—sparked

between his fingers where he touched her.

But this flame was not orange or red, or even ochre as most flames were.

No, this flame was *black*, its center a bright, shimmering blue.

Like the ribbons of magic from the diviner...

The sound of doors shutting echoed in the cavernous space, and Isabelle knew they were alone.

"I'd like that," he said softly, his voice betraying the weakness he must have been feeling.

Isabelle leaned into his touch, feeling it truly for the first time.

And just like magic, the sparks of fire soothed her soul, quelling the heat as it had when she'd kissed him all those nights ago at the party.

Spike slowly ambled into a room that boasted not much more than a solid, circular bed surrounded by clear, floor to ceiling windows. A fire burned bright and red, illuminating the room amidst several votives lined on the mantle, and the scent of burning sage was potent.

"Didn't peg you as the occultist type," she said nervously as Spike collapsed on the bed. He pulled his knees to his chest, pursing his lips and squinting his eyes.

She could tell he was in pain, and the sight caused the radiating pain in her chest to return.

The sound of his blood rushing in her ears was like a drum, his heartbeat a blaring guitar solo.

"I'm not, but Cate's wheelhouse is magic. Though, I don't think there's any herbs or spell that can fix me, but I appreciate her trying."

Isabelle bit her lip as she sat down on the bed, leaving a modicum of space between them.

"I'm so sorry Spike, I didn't... I didn't know my venom would do this to you, I—"

"I did. I knew."

"Then why..."

"I haven't been completely honest with you, Iz," he said as he coughed, the sound racking his body. He looked like death.

"I was cursed. To be a hellhound for eternity. No one, least of all me, expected to ever be human again, but that day at the cafe... your presence triggered my shift."

Isabelle scooted closer, involuntarily

setting her hand on his thigh. The touch warmed her in a way that both soothing and invigorating.

"Spike..."

"Let me finish," he said as he coughed again, clearing his throat.

"Cate and Hades took me to see the Fates. They told me that unless I received a kiss and a bite of death from my *mate,* I would cease to be human and I would turn back into a hellhound, forever."

Isabelle's heart sank, a mixture of emotion flooding her.

Sadness, anger.

Understanding.

"That's why you bit me," she said as tears threatened to fall from her eyes.

"No, I mean... yes, but it was more than that. I should have... I should have told you the truth, but I was afraid you'd run away..."

"And take your chance at humanity with me," she said, sniffling like a child.

She wanted to be strong, but the pain in her body, the heat that was causing her to feel like an inflamed volcano, was making stability quite difficult. Not to mention the man in front of her who looked two steps away from death itself.

"I spent my whole life waiting to live it," he said as he closed his eyes.

"And then I found you, and I just... didn't want to lose *you* along with it. No one ever felt right, not like you do. Not to mention, I'm a bit of a freak of nature if you haven't noticed," he said as he took a deep breath. His eyes watered, his breath coming in rapid pants.

"You're not a freak of nature," she

said as she leaned in closer, needing to touch him, to soothe his soul despite her own feelings about his admission.

To make his pain stop...

"Before I met you, Isabelle, I was a cursed, virginal hellhound with a fucking knot."

"You were a... what now?" she asked, her dress clinging to her skin as the heat flared beneath her skin. It reminded her of the first time she'd touched him, her heat so intense she'd needed a cold shower just to get back to neutral.

But his words were not lost on her.

"The other night when we..." She swallowed nervously.

Spike gazed back at her, with a longing and awe that cut her to the core.

"It all happened so fast, but I don't regret it. I know I should, but I don't regret anything about you, Isabelle. You make me hungry. You make me want to take this life by the throat and then some. You were my first, and you'll be my only. It's my fate, to be yours," he said, his gaze never breaking hers.

"So I bit you. I marked you because my hound and my human couldn't bear the thought of anyone else taking you," he said as he closed his eyes. His chest rose and fell softly, his breath shallow.

Because he was *dying.*

Without her bite, he would surely die from the venom in his blood, the venom that was poisoning him.

Isabelle lurched forward, pulling him into her arms. He felt light as a feather in her hold.

"I wasn't honest with you either, Spike," she said shakily.

"I didn't understand this bond," she started. "I was dying, when I was bitten," she said as she ran a sweaty hand through his damn hair.

His golden eyes held her gaze like she was the sun.

"And for years, I thought my penance was the lives I took to sustain myself. But I never wanted to hurt people, just as I never wanted to hurt you." She felt a sob ransack her chest as Spike settled his hand over hers.

"I thought I could change, I thought... I thought the way back to humanity for me was to stop being what I am. That's why I came here, to USC. To find who I was beneath the blood and the hunt, and instead, I—"

The words on the edge of her tongue would never be taken back after she said them, and that should have scared her.

But as she looked into the eyes of her *mate*, she knew there were things far worse to fear than the truth.

She'd waited her whole life to be *loved*, not as a monster, but as the woman she was.

For someone with an equal zest for life, an equal fighting spirit.

Someone who would fight for *her*.

"You make me hungry too, Spike, and that is as terrifying as it is amazing," she said as he stared back at her wind wonder.

"Isabelle, I—"

Isabelle could hold off no more. She gingerly removed his collar, brought her lips to his without haste, tasting the salt of his sweat, and the hunger in his kiss.

Spike kissed her back delicately,

sincerely. His fingers gripped her hair, his grip tight as he held on for what felt like dear life.

"Izzy..." he whispered, his breath catching in his throat. "I can't breathe, I—"

The world faded as her fangs pushed forth.

She knew what she needed to do, and for the first time in her long life, she was not afraid.

For this was what she was *born to do.*

To bite, to bond.

Isabelle licked the salty flesh of his neck, his faint pulse echoing beneath his clammy skin. She slid her arm up his back and she pulled him to her lips, his bated breath full of fear and love.

Full of lust.

"I'm sorry, Spike, I should have done

this sooner," she murmured as she sank her teeth into his flesh.

Spike cried out in pain, his fingers tightening their grip almost to the point of pain as he thrashed about in her grip. His breathing hitched, his body shook, and his *claws* extended against her skull.

Isabelle did not relent, she drank him down like he was water and she was dying of thirst. And perhaps she was, because nothing and no one would ever taste as delicious as her mate.

Not now, not ever again.

Bright blue magic erupted from between them. The fire flickered before dying out completely, and the sound of bulbs breaking echoed in the spacious house.

Spike had gone limp in her arms.

Isabelle raised her head, licking the blood from her lips. He did not move.

"Spike..." she called as she shook him. His silence was a fate worse than death.

"Spike, say something..." she said as she brushed the hair from his eyes. The only light was that of the blue energy that surrounded them.

"Spike!" she said as tears poured forth from her eyes.

CHAPTER NINETEEN

ALL AT ONCE, the heat *stopped*. The blood in his veins slowed to a steady flow, and his muscles strengthened. There was no need to shift, no hunger, no longing.

There was only the feel of her fingernails digging into his skin, of his heartbeat thudding away.

The fire around him did not burn or hurt, instead it was a residual calm.

"I'm too late," he said, his voice soft amidst the crackle of the fire.

A shadow emerged from the flames. The form sharpened into his vision, and he could see the lumbering, ominous shape was not a person.

It was an animal.

The hellhound sat on its haunches, its beady red eyes staring back at Spike, it's metal spikes on its collar glinting from the light of the fire.

This is who he was, who he'd been for ages.

And it wasn't a terrible existence. He'd grown comfortable in Cate's care. He was never starved for food or attention, and he enjoyed the peace and solitude that came with living on the edge of society, after all those years of reaping and hunting, of death.

But as he stared at the hound's sleek black coat, his bright red eyes... he knew that the rest of his journey would have to be walked alone.

He kneeled to the hound, reaching his hand out to scratch behind his ears.

"We've had a lot of years together, haven't we, boy?" he said softly.

The hound leaned into his palm.

Magic danced around his fingertips. Blue flames and white-blue ribbons danced together like a double helix.

"But you can't come with me," he said, his voice full of pain and despair.

"Spike!" Isabelle's voice sounded far away, but it also sounded... scared.

Why was she scared?

Spike ran his hand down the hound's head, his hands settling on his collar.

When he moved his hand away, he

saw blood. Dark, crimson blood stained the metal, and a sharp pain radiated in his chest.

It felt like someone was pounding on his chest.

The hound whined as he stood, a sense of urgency overcoming him. In the distance he could see the darkness, the oncoming night.

It was frightening, cold, and he was not certain he'd make it through.

"No no no... you can't die, not like this, not after I..."

Die? I'm right here...

The hound nudged his leg, whimpering.

I'll always be here, if you need me.

The words echoed in his brain, and he knew they were not his own. They belonged to the beast within him.

Spike scratched the hound's ears. "I know," he said softly as he dropped his hand, glancing at the shadowed horizon.

Spike turned to take one last look at the creature, before he took a step forward. Out of the fire and warmth, he trudged into the dark, frozen space of the unknown, following the sound of Isabelle's voice.

He hated to hear her so frightened, so upset.

It's okay, Izzy, I'm coming...

His heartbeat stilled as he stared at the blue magic, swirling around a circular door. He turned to see the fire had died to embers, and the hound was no more than a faint shadow.

Spike took a step forward bravely, knowing that in his heart on the other side of the darkness was the light.

His body shifted as he gasped for air, sitting upright. Fingertips squeezed his neck, the motion a bit sharp as if he had fresh wounds...

"Why are you screaming?" he said as he caught his breath, his face buried in soft, strawberry blonde hair.

Isabelle pulled him away for a moment, looking at him with tear-stained cheeks.

"You're alive... you—"

"Of course I'm alive, you—"

Isabelle crushed her lips to his, and he could taste the sweet, tang of blood.

My blood, he realized.

Isabelle bit me... she...

She saved me.

Spike's shoulders loosened as he settled his hand in her hair, pulling her closer. His muscles felt a renewed vigor, his strength coming back to him tenfold. He pulled Isabelle into his lap, running his hands up her thighs, beneath her dress. Her skin was warm from the heat between them, slick with the remains of her cold sweat. His fingers bunched at her dress, and she lifted her arms without order, letting him undress her. The cold air kissed her skin, eliciting goosebumps on her pale breasts. His cock strained against his jeans, as he took in the sight of her. Bloody lips and fangs, crimson eyes, golden hair falling haphazardly around her shoulders, out of her ponytail. Swollen breasts caged behind black lace, heaving with rapid breath.

Isabelle Costanza was dangerous, beautiful, and undeniably *his*.

"You saved me," he whispered as he

wiped some blood from the corner of her mouth. Spike ran his hand down her neck, resting his palm there as he gazed back at her.

"No, Spike, I think... we saved each other," she said as she leaned her forehead against his, capturing his mouth in a sweet, tender kiss. Her fingertips trailed tiny touches of fire along his cheek, down his neck, and as she stroked the expanse of skin, he realized he was without collar.

The anxiety he'd once felt about removing it died in the darkness that surrounded them as he slid his hand over hers,

He could finally *breathe*, because he was free.

Free of the curse, of an animal's instincts.

And there was only one thing he wanted, one thing he needed now and forevermore.

Isabelle.

Spike kissed her back, trailing his lips along the skin of her neck, licking the semi-healed wounds he'd left in her skin.

"Spike..." she groaned as he let his tongue lavish her sweet skin.

Isabelle's hands made swift motions at his belt, the sound of the metal clicking against the hold like chimes blown by the wind.

"Yes, my love?" he murmured softly against her skin, the words free and full for the first time.

He felt no fear, no worry about how she would react, or if she would run.

Not now, not ever again.

"Need... you... burning up," she said, her voice full of the same hazy lust it held the first time they'd done this.

He made quick work of removing her bra, watching as her bountiful breasts fell from their fabric cage. He did not wait to take one, pert nipple into his mouth, letting his fangs graze the tender flesh.

Isabelle let out a sound that was something between a whisper and a moan, a sound that make his cock throb as he ground his aching erection against her, eliciting another deep whisper-moan from her lips.

"I need you too, Iz," he said as he slid his hand beneath her moist panties. He let his fingers tickle and trace the edges of her slick lips, taking her already swollen clit between his thumb and forefinger.

"Please..." Isabelle moaned as she thrust herself against his torturous fingers as she freed his cock, pushing down his jeans and underwear just below his ass. "I don't know if I can stand this much longer..." she breathed.

Spike stopped his motions for a moment as he shifted them both, if only so he could shake off the constraints of his pants.

Isabelle scooted back on the bed, giving him room. The lights flickered above them, as the fire raged in the fireplace.

Spike watched as Isabelle's gaze fell over him where he stood, taking him in from head to knot to toe as she slid her panties off.

"Gods, you are so much better than

any monster romance," she murmured, her hand sliding across her abdomen, down toward her glistening lips.

"I am yours," he said as he kneeled on the bed, palming his cock. His knot was already swollen, moisture already pebbling at the tip of his cock as he took in the sight of his mate, wet and wanting.

"Tell me what you want, Isabelle," he said as he crawled over to her slowly, his gaze never breaking hers.

"Tell me what you want, and I will give it to you," he whispered as he settled himself over top of her, the tip of his cock brushing just the edge of her entrance.

Isabelle stared up at him with blood red eyes, licking her swollen, pink lips as she said, "I want you, Spike. I want you and your knot to make me see stars," she said with heavy breath.

"But I also want to give *you* the things *you* need," she said as she took his face in her hands. "Tell me what you want, Spike."

CHAPTER TWENTY

THE WORDS IN the air were heavy as Isabelle's heart beat faster.

Spike licked his lips, the sight causing a fresh influx of moisture to blossom between her thighs. His dark gaze held hers, but it was more than just lustful. It was also full of understanding, compassion, and hope.

She ran her thumb over his cheek as she fought to grind her aching pussy against the head of his cock, which was poised painstakingly just outside of her entrance.

Because as badly as she wanted him—and she did want him and his full, swollen knot like a desert wants the rain—she wanted to give him *everything* no one else had ever given him.

While Isabelle hadn't regretted their salacious romp in the dungeon, Spike's admission that it was his *first time* made her feel a bit guilty, despite the fact he seemed to have quite the capability, despite his inexperience, to bring her *multiple* orgasms.

But the act itself had been rather... rushed, and she did not wish to do so again. She wanted to give Spike what she hadn't been able to give him that night in the dungeon.

Control.

"I want to feel you," he whispered in her ear, his lips kissing the skin just beneath it as he trailed his fingers down once more, teasing her entrance.

"Spike..." she groaned, unable to resist thrusting her hips against his relentless fingers.

"I want to hear you call my name like that," he whispered again as he slid another finger inside her warm entrance, increasing his rhythm. "When I make you come."

The pace was agonizingly slow, and Isabelle moaned in frustration.

Spike gazed down at her as he slid another finger in, and Isabelle could not contain herself or her orgasm that hit out of nowhere. She cried his name as her insides fluttered as he pulled his fingers out.

"I want to taste you," he said as he slowly, trailing his way down her body, sliding his hands underneath her thighs, lifting her to his mouth.

The onslaught of his tongue pushing through her pulsing loins was too much.

She tightened her legs around his head, her fingers reaching out to tangle in the sheets on the bed as the fire burned brighter, like a beacon in the night.

"You taste like strawberries and cream," he murmured his fangs nipping at her sensitive bead.

"Spike..." She rolled her head to the side as his tongue licked a long, sinful line from her lips to her navel, as he crawled back up her body.

He positioned himself above her, his

golden eyes staring down at her with such wonder and awe, it nearly shattered her to a million pieces.

"I want to feel you in every part of me, for the rest of my immortal life," he whispered as he kissed her slowly.

She could taste herself on his tongue, and while she did not think it was anything similar to strawberries, she could not deny it wasn't unpleasant.

Isabelle hooked her legs around Spike's hip, pulling him closer.

Spike rolled his hips in tandem, the motion drawing him into her at last with wordless ease.

There was no hunger, no heat, no pain.

No otherworldly desire or need, no torturous touch.

There was only the coolness of cold

sweat, the soft caress of skin, and the faint sound of breath and the crackle of the fire.

Isabelle slid her hands up over his hips, trailing her fingertips up his spine.

Spike tore his lips from hers, peppering kisses along her slender neck.

Isabelle let out a sound of contentment at the sensation of his lips on her skin meddling with the feel of his swollen knot stretching her. There was only a slight movement as he drew his hips back, but there was no exit, for his knot had hit its peak, and they were well and truly *locked* in place.

Such a thing should have alarmed her, but it did not. Instead, it filled her with a bliss she'd always read about, but never known.

Isabelle pressed her lips against

Spike's neck, licking the pink, fresh holes before sinking her fangs back into him.

"Isabelle," he groaned as the pace of his thrust started to become more erratic.

"Spike," she murmured as fresh blood coated her tongue. It was sweeter than anything she'd ever tasted.

The sharpness of fangs in her own neck was a blissful sort of pain, and she couldn't help but gasp at the sensation.

Spike's warm tongue licked at the fresh bite, lapping up the blood as she met his chaotic pace, following him thorough the fire and into heaven.

Spike took her bloody lips like a prayer as blinding bliss surrounded them, and Isabelle thought she could have died in his kiss. A sudden burst of warmth filled her insides as his cock pulsed within her, pushing her over the edge.

"Mine," he whispered against her lips as he slowly thrust into her once more before stilling completely.

Exhaustion hit like a brick as they both came down from splintering heights, all the energy, magic, and emotion too much to bear.

Spike slowly made his exit, but the warmth he'd filled her with remained all throughout her body, marking her from the inside out.

And when Isabelle curled closer into Spike's fire and brimstone scent, she let herself fall.

And as Spike trailed his fingers up and down her back, the rise and fall of his chest lulled her into a peaceful slumber.

CHAPTER TWENTY-ONE

SPIKE CASUALLY STROLLED through the Leehan Gallery, taking in the final sight of the exhibit before him. He still couldn't believe there had almost been a chance he wouldn't have seen it.

It seemed wild to him that only days ago he was on death's proverbial door, fading from the toxic vampire venom in his blood. Venom that could only be stabilized by the bite of death itself, or rather, a venomous mate bite.

The fact Hades had taken it upon himself to find Isabelle made Spike feel more than indebted to the once-God.

Though Hades had told him, there was no debt to be paid whatsoever—especially since he was now mortal—and instead insisted that it had *always* been his job to take care of those that belonged to him.

Including Spike.

There was still much uncertainty abound with what the future held for him as well as his guardians—his chosen family—but for now, Spike was more than content to live moment to moment. Where his life once before had been an endless string of days trapped as a hellish beast, now there was only the unexpected, the surprise of what lay forth, every day different than the last.

A delicate hand slid around his waist before the warmth overtook him.

The fire of his bond with Isabelle had—as Hades has spoken of—burned off. Though that did not mean that Spike's lust or his hunger to consume his vampire mate had diminished by any means. In fact, his desire was as untethered as he was. Free from the collar and leash that once controlled him, the hellish heat had settled to a steady, crackling fire. One that could always rise from the ashes. And rise it did, every time he looked at her.

And he knew it would always be like that. There was so much to see, to do, to explore with this woman who instilled a deep hunger in him to taste the world at their feet and spend the rest of forever in eternal discovery.

"Come on, we're going to be late for our reservation at the Cafe," she purred, her hands sliding up and down his stomach as she swayed back and forth.

"I just... it's hard to wrap my head around the fact that only a few days ago I was..."

"I know," Isabelle said as she pulled away, sliding her hand in between his fingers instead,

"You aren't the only one who's been thrown for a loop," she said as she tugged on his hand. The feeling sent tiny shockwaves through his palm and wrist, reminding him of the fire between them. The proof that they were made for one another...

"Lorelei's been acting all sorts of strange lately, I think this whole vampires are real-hellfire bond thing is getting to her too, even if she doesn't say anything," Isabelle admitted. "Not to mention Eric is pretty much chomping at the bit to be in the room with Daddy Hades again," she smirked. "I think he might have a crush." She giggled.

Spike rolled his eyes, shaking his head.

"You can not under any circumstances let him know we call him that," Spike responded, squeezing her hand.

"I suppose you are right, we probably should get going..." he said as he smiled at her.

"I've only checked the doors and locks, like, three times."

"It'll be fine, I promise," she said as she tugged his hand,

"I just... I can't help but feel like this sense of *déjà vu* or something. Like the minute we leave, it's all going to go hell in a handbasket or something,"

"Are you two done closing up?' Lorelai's voice carried down the hall.

"Yeah, yeah, Spike was just doing his triple check..." Isabelle said.

Spike ran his free hand through his hair.

Perhaps I am just being paranoid...

"Come on, I'm starving..." Isabelle said, licking her lips and fangs.

Spike's cock twitched immediately at the sight, a wicked grin forming on his face.

"Me too, but I don't think the DeLux Cafe has what I'm craving," he said.

Isabelle rolled her eyes as she pulled him down the hall, and he followed her like a moth to a flame.

Isabelle turned to look at him over her shoulder as she dropped his hand, a smirk gracing her lips.

"Last one to the car is buying," she said as she took off with a laugh.

Spike shook his head as he took off in a sprint, chasing the laughing vampire down the shadowed hallway, her intoxicating scent of roses and lilies awakening the animal inside of him once more.

It did not take long for Spike to catch his prey, and a part of him rationalized perhaps his mate enjoyed being caught and prayed upon.

He lifted Isabelle in his arms with swift motion before she'd made it to the car, where Lorelai and Eric were standing.

Isabelle twisted in his grasp, but his hold was tight as he kissed her victoriously.

"I'm pretty sure that's not in the rules," she said as she relaxed in his hold.

"I am pretty sure we make our own rules now," he said as he set her gently back on her feet.

Isabelle shook her head.

"You are going to be the death of me, Spike Moon," she said as Lorelai and Eric piled into the car.

"I'm counting on it, Isabelle," Spike responded as he opened the car door for her, kissing her as if it was the first and the last time he'd ever do so.

And together they burned like hellfire; bright, beautiful, and forevermore.

Thank you for reading Spike!

If you enjoyed this book, please return to the retailer and leave a review. Your words mean so much and help us to continue writing the books you love.

Follow our Facebook page
Speed Dating with the Denizens of the Underworld Series

Watch your favorite online retailer for the other books in the Speed Dating with the Denizens of the Underworld series.

Watch for the other books in the
Speed Dating with the Denizens of the
Underworld Series

Lucifer

Ash

Azrael

Samael

Azazel

Hecate

Bastet

Cain

Thor

Demi

Hell's Belle

Arachne

Osiris

Hades

Lilith

Adam

SPIKE

Loki

Orion

Cassiel

Hera

Asterion

Seth

Triton

Michael

Alastor

Athena

Zeus

Baal

Fenrir

Medusa

Raphael

Spike

Gabrielle

Calliope

Artemis

And More!

OTHER BOOKS BY ARIEL DAWN

The Hunter Games

Blood Of My Enemy

Blood Of The Lost

Thorne Of Blood

Speed Dating with the Denizens of the Underworld Series

Hecate

Hades

Orion

Athena

Spike

The Forevermore Series

In The Cards

In The Blood

SPIKE

In The Shadows

In The Deep

In The Garden

In The Night

Shifters Of Starfall Creek Series

Hollow's Sunrise

Hollow's Sunset

Hollow's Legacy

Shifters of Starfall Creek Collection:

Books 1-3

Sign up for Ariel Dawn's newsletter and
claim your sweet treat!
https://view.flodesk.com/pages/64b2b6
efe181ddda00ff2a1e

CONNECT WITH ARIEL DAWN

Website

http://www.ariel-dawn.com/

Goodreads:

http://www.goodreads.com/authorariel

dawn

Bookbub:

http://www.bookbub.com/authors/ariel

-dawn

Facebook:

http://www.facebook.com/authorarielda

wn

Twitter:

https://twitter.com/ArielDawn10

Join Dusk Chasers—Ariel Dawn's Official Readers Group for access to exclusive content! https://www.facebook.com/groups/689167388350361

ABOUT ARIEL DAWN

USA TODAY BESTSELLING AUTHOR Ariel Dawn grew up as an avid reader and is a creative soul.

What started out as writing reviews for indie romance authors led to featuring quirky, stereotypical, and weird covers on her Instagram Wrong Turn Romance, which gave her the courage to finally decide to live her dream and become an author.

Ariel writes plot driven paranormal romance and hopes to venture into fantasy and rom-com in the future. When she isn't writing, she can be found cosplaying, attending conventions, creating all sorts of artwork in her studio, or editing photos for her photography business.

A self-professed geek and foodie, she loves hanging out with family and friends and playing video games and board games with her retro gamer husband.